DEAR NEIGHBOR

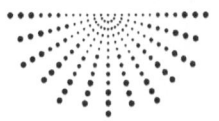

RIVER LAURENT

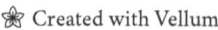 Created with Vellum

For
Brittany Urbaniak
You are simply amazing!
Hope I can be as great for you one day.

"FUCK"

One of the most interesting words in the English language today is the word 'fuck'. It is one magical word: just by its sound it can describe pain, pleasure, hate and love. In language, it falls into many grammatical categories. It can be used as a verb, both transitive (John fucked Mary) and intransitive (Mary was fucked by John), and as a noun (Mary is a fine fuck). It can be used as an adjective (Mary is fucking beautiful). As you can see there are not many words with the versatility of 'fuck'.

Besides the sexual meaning, there are also the following uses:

Fraud: I got fucked at the used car lot.

Ignorance: Fucked if I know.

Trouble: I guess I am fucked now!

Aggression: Fuck you!

Displeasure: What the fuck is going on here?

Difficulty: I can't understand this fucking job.

Incompetence: He is a fuck-off.

Suspicion: What the fuck are you doing?

Enjoyment: I had a fucking good time.

Request: Get the fuck out of here!

Hostility: I am going to knock your fucking head off!
Greeting: How the fuck are you?
Apathy: Who gives a fuck?
Innovation: Get a bigger fucking hammer.
Surprise: Fuck! You scared the shit out of me!
Anxiety: Today is really fucked.

- Osho(1980)

1

MIMI

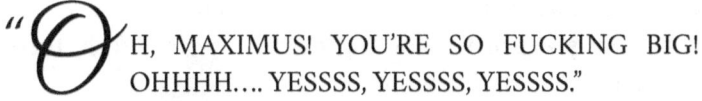

"OH, MAXIMUS! YOU'RE SO FUCKING BIG! OHHHH…. YESSSS, YESSSS, YESSSS."

I opened my eyes.

Seriously? At the crack of dawn? Didn't these people need to sleep? At all?

What kind of name was Maximus, anyway?

I punched my pillow aggressively and burrowed under it while the screamer moved into the high-pitched segment of her climax. It really was quite incredible how thin these walls were.

Although, I hadn't noticed as much bedroom activity next door when all my other neighbors were still living here. I used to hear TVs, radios, doors slamming shut, children screaming, and the odd domestic squabble, but since the Great Exodus started nine months ago, the corridors had slowly fallen silent. Sometimes, I imagined myself as a survivor of some apocalyptic event. The only girl in the world, living on her own.

Well, not entirely on her own.

I had one other holdout on my floor. The only other person unwilling to give in to the sight of dollar signs. I didn't know how much the neighbors who left were offered for their homes, but they were practically jumping out their windows into their moving trucks. One by one, I'd watched them go. Until only two of us were left.

Me and Sex God.

My one-bedroom apartment was just slightly bigger than a chocolate box, but it was as cute as a button, and in the ridiculously expensive housing market of New York, there was nothing not to like about it.

The noises from next door had stopped so I dug myself out from under my pillows. The room was filled with sunlight. It was not quite the crack of dawn, after all. I was not a morning person. I like my sleep in the mornings, every goddamned second of it. I squinted at the alarm clock. It was not due to ring for another half-an-hour. It felt as if my eyelids had just started to drift down again when the damn thing rang.

I slammed my hand down on it.

Muttering curses at my neighbor for ruining my sleep, I dragged myself away from my lovely bed. And my bed was a very lovely place. Silk sheets from Italy, Siberian goose down-filled duvet and pillows, antique damask bedspread from England. Yeah, my bed was my greatest indulgence.

I stumbled to the bathroom and landed on the toilet seat. As I reach for the roll of toilet paper, I heard flushing from my neighbor's apartment. Probably flushing down used condoms, at least five, I thought sourly.

By the time I had brushed my teeth; my fury at my neighbor's nocturnal activities stealing my sleep had abated. At this time of the morning, there was only one thing on my mind: coffee.

I was passing through the living room on my way to the kitchen when my gaze fell on an envelope lying on the floor next to my front door. The insignia on the envelope and the large PRIVATE & CONFIDENTIAL stamp was unmistakable. It was another letter from the law firm of Noble, Noble, and Flaherty. Since all mail was dropped off downstairs they must have sent one of their little minions by to hand-deliver it.

First thing in the morning and before coffee! I felt my anger and resentment rise again. The persistence and nerve of these people. Thinking that everyone had their price.

Wondering what the new offer would be, I snatched it off the floor and tore it open. When I caught sight of the amount my mind went blank.

"Son of a bitch," I whispered. My knees were suddenly so weak I had to sink down on the piano stool by the door. Holy crap. Wow, ripping out small apartments and converting them into luxury homes and penthouses for super-rich big shots must be a really profitable business.

I was staring at a figure that had to be twice what my apartment was worth—no, probably more than that. With that amount of money, I could find an even bigger place, go on vacation, buy that dreamy bed from Liberty, add to my collection of pillows…

I turned on the stool I was sitting on until I faced the upright piano. I ran my fingers over the keys. Having absolutely no musical talent I never could master the instrument, but I could play a couple of old tunes.

My two index fingers met in the middle and began to tap furiously. Chopsticks. I remembered my grandmother laughing. The sound of her laughter was like an echo from the past. All the hours I'd spent sitting on that stool with her came back to me. Even though she knew I didn't have a musical bone in my body she never stopped believing in me.

2

MIMI

When I was a kid, this apartment belonged to my grandmother. When things turned sour between my parents, I'd come here rather than spend the weekends in our home, where all my parents seemed to do was fight and snipe at each other.

My grandmother must have known I was coming to her to escape my parents' bickering, but she always behaved as if my arrival was the best surprise on the planet. She was beyond thrilled to have me, no matter how many times I showed up at her door. Eventually, I even had my own set of keys.

Then, when she was dying in the hospital she told me she had willed her home to me, even though my mother was her rightful heir. When I tried to tell her that she would be hurting her own daughter, she firmly told me it was her last wish and I must respect it.

No, I wouldn't give this place up for anything. I didn't need a handcrafted bed from Liberty to be happy. And I already had a dozen unused pillows stuffed away in my cupboards. Who needs vacations when my whole life at the moment felt like a vacation? No, this apartment meant more to me than all the money in the world.

I had already written two long letters telling those blood-sucking lawyers representing those faceless, soulless corporations that, but obviously, they either didn't get the message or didn't want to get it. They almost had enough to buy out almost an entire building full of hardworking people, but not quite. Me and Sex God next door, we couldn't be bought.

Since polite replies stating that the apartment was mine legally and I would never let it go, didn't work, I grabbed a pen and scribbled across the signature area:

KISS MY ASS!

*A*nd look, they were thoughtful enough to include a return envelope, stamped and everything. I took a little too much pleasure in sealing my response inside. Feeling like I'd fought a battle and won, I slid the envelope into my purse to be mailed on my way to work and went to the kitchen to make myself a strong mug of coffee.

I showered in my large, claw foot tub. I mean, come on. Who wouldn't kill for that? I was extraordinarily blessed and lucky. I laughed a little as I shampooed my hair. The developers were welcome to keep on trying; I would never give up my home. Why would I? Actually, I was secretly glad the idiots had to keep paying their obviously expensive lawyers to send me their offer letters. It would be interesting to see what figure they would go to before they finally gave up and built their fancy apartments around me?

Draped in a fluffy towel, I padded back into my pretty blue and white bedroom. I pulled out a pink blouse and paired it with a sexy, charcoal wraparound skirt. Sitting at my vanity, I curled my chocolatey hair into big, bouncy curls that fell all around my face and neck. I added mascara and slicked on a layer of strawberry flavored gloss. I pointed the gloss wand at my reflection. "You're pretty fabulous, Mimi Young. Don't you forget it."

I threw open my shoe cupboard and sighed with pleasure. It was more like a shrine to the top shoe designers in the world than a shoe cupboard. Rows and rows of beautiful shoes. One-hundred and ninety-eight to be exact. The best ones were on the top three shelves. Other people invested in art; I invested in shoes. From the middle of the shelf, I picked up a pair of skin-toned, three-inch high pumps. I slipped into them and immediately felt like a million dollars.

Walking to the full-length mirror, I blew myself a kiss before hurrying out the door. Of course, I was running late. My little trip down memory lane at the piano had taken too much time. I stepped out into the empty hallway, walked briskly down to the elevator and jammed my finger against the button. The car carriage began its ascent upwards. I looked around me. It was like living in the middle of a ghost town. I was almost always alone. Almost.

I heard a door opening and a woman laugh.

3

MIMI

*S*hit! The shag-fest next door must be over. My neighbor and his screamer were on their walk of shame. I looked up at the lighted numbers above the elevator doors as the lift slowly chugged its way up to the top floor.

Behind me, the woman giggled.

Come on, I silently urged. If the elevator arrived in the next few seconds, I could nip in and close the doors before they got here.

But of course, the old, decrepit thing refused to play ball. I must have been downwind, or something because I could smell Sex God's aftershave as he approached. I tried to calm myself, but meanwhile, heat rose through me and my palms started to sweat.

I might have forgotten to mention earlier that Sex God was also almost supernaturally gorgeous. In the past year, I'd seen him about half a dozen times and each time he looked like he'd just walked out of someone's sex dream.

Tall, broad-shouldered, with dark hair, that he would occasionally brush back off his forehead. He also had sensual lips that I once saw him licking, an unbearably sexy chin dimple, and piercing gray eyes that could hypnotize a cobra. He wore tailored suits the way women wore lingerie, knowing it made him look edible. He could have been a model.

Maybe he was, for all I knew, since I choked up and became unable to utter a single word whenever he was around. For his part, he barely looked in my direction. Made sense. Square-jawed, super-hot guys were generally stuck-up assholes. They didn't need to be sweet or friendly to get laid. He seemed to fit the bill nicely.

The first time I saw him, was maybe a year earlier when he first moved into the largest apartment on my floor. Poor hunk, I naively thought, just as he settled in. Those monsters from Noble, Noble, and Flaherty were trying to edge him out. But like me, he held fast. I was glad that he'd told them where to put their offer. Since we were in the same boat, I thought I would introduce myself. Stupid me, thinking we had something in common.

I smiled at him the next time I saw him and he looked me up and down with the sort of expression people usually had when they smelled something bad. It was almost enough to make me take a sniff of myself, just in case. But no. It wasn't me. It was him being a raging jerk. One little nod, then he turned away. I bit my tongue before I could ask him what the hell his problem was.

A tanned hand reached out to hit the button for the underground parking garage, and my eyes were drawn by a strange magnetic power upward along his immaculately tailored sleeve past those wonderful pecs and golden throat to his face. Since he seemed to be entranced by the lighted numbers above the doors, I couldn't help it. My gaze took a trip down to his crotch. Yes, there was definitely something very big down there.

The screamer's response to my eye flick was instantaneous.

She laid her claim by moving closer to him and draping her hand over his arm. Our eyes met. Hers were smug. She was what you'd expect, blonde, beautiful, and skinny, although the word I prefer is 'bitch'. I calmly shifted my gaze to the lighted numbers and refrained from telling her that Sex God preferred quantity over quality. I doubted she would be coming around again.

The lift doors opened with laborious slowness.

Gray eyes trained on me. "After you."

His gravelly, deep voice melted its way down my back. I stepped into the lift and stared straight ahead as they came in and the doors closed. The journey down was a bit of an ordeal. No one spoke. The shrew threw me dirty looks and I fought the urge not to fidget.

Finally, after what seemed like hours later, the torture ended. The lift jerked and doors slowly creaked open at ground level. I was in such a rush I nearly tumbled out. I didn't hang around long enough to hear the doors close behind me. The pair could have carried on down to the depths of hell for all I cared.

4

MIMI

I picked up an egg white sandwich and a skinny soy latte from my local café and rushed through the revolving doors of Jett & Stone Investments. Flying through the glass, chrome, and granite foyer I just managed to squeeze into the lift before it closed.

My boss, Josh wouldn't be around this morning. He was meeting some clients. A smile came to my lips as I thought of him. After two years of working here, we became a 'thing' last month.

Yeah, I know. I was sleeping with the boss.

Not officially, obviously, because of office gossip and uncomfortable situations, but we were both going at it like rabbits. It started one day while we were working late. He turned his head and suddenly kissed me.

The earth didn't move, or anything like that, but it was more than nice, and it made me realize how long it had been since I had been with a man. Josh was quite good-looking with a slim athletic body. His fingernails were always clean and he didn't live too far away from me. Not a bad catch.

The lift doors opened at floor fourteen and I walked briskly into the Private Equity department. The good thing about showing up late on a Monday morning was not being the only one. I could sort of blend in with the rest of the shifty-eyed latecomers and get to my desk without too much notice.

Nobody blinked an eye as I made my way down the narrow glass corridor and slipped into my cubicle. I booted up my computer, and to make it look like I'd been there for a while I placed my sandwich and latte on my desk and strategically scattered some paperwork around them.

By the time my computer came on, it looked like I'd been there for ages. The first thing I always did on Monday morning was to tackle my inbox. It would be full of a week-end's worth of emails from clients, both happy and less-than, and if I didn't clear them, piles of new emails would get dumped on top of them, which I hated, but since I had the unenviable task of preparing for a status meeting at half-past twelve I decided to do it after I finished my notes for the meeting.

I worked on my notes for two hours solid then started on my emails.

We'd recently launched a new version of our online access portal. It was supposed to allow clients to get into their state-ments day or night. Most of my emails appeared to be from clients requesting help accessing their accounts.

I sighed and opened the first one. The email icon blinked at the top left-hand corner of my screen and I smiled. Josh. He must be back if he was sending me an email. I looked around to be sure nobody was looking over my shoulder before opening it.

Guess what I thought about all weekend long? The way you taste. Your smell, and those little mewing, kitten sounds you make when I eat you out.

I grinned and craned my neck to see into his office. He had his shirt sleeves rolled up and was talking to Drake from Accounting. I dropped my eyes back to the screen.

I wish I had been with you this weekend instead of with my parents. All I did was walk around trying to hide a hard-on because I couldn't stop thinking about your pussy.

I can't wait to devour you tonight.

The whole time I was pretending to listen to those asses downtown, I was imagining you under my desk sucking me off.

Hope you're wearing your red thong!

Josh xx

I blew out a long, slow breath. Oh, Josh, you dirty dog you, but in fact, I was wearing a red thong. Once I knew it was his thing—he liked tearing it off with his teeth—I ordered two dozen from the internet. I pictured him between my legs, humming to himself as he ate me out, and started to feel warm and tingly. Yes, Josh sure knew what I wanted, and how I wanted it.

I enjoyed my relationship with Josh. Maybe it was because we had worked with each other for so long I felt I really knew him. Unlike my manwhore neighbor, he could be completely trusted.

Of course, my bestie, Megan, was dead set against the idea of me and Josh. In her books, sleeping with the boss was always a recipe for disaster, but I told her it would be all right since he wasn't exactly my direct boss. I quoted one of my grandmother's favorite sayings to her: stop buying trouble before it goes on sale.

I reread his dirty email. We hadn't been together since Thursday night at my place. That's three days without sex while Josh visited his parents in Schenectady. I was just as eager to be devoured by him as he was to devour me.

I hit "Reply," then typed:

Dear Josh,

If absolutely necessary I can tentatively pencil you into my diary for a good sucking under the desk after lunch. Please confirm a time that would suit you.

Best regards.

Mimi xx

Smiling to myself, I hit 'Send'.

5

MIMI

*A*t the precise instant I clicked send, another email titled URGENT from someone called Lillian Taylor appeared at the top left-hand corner of my screen. Later I would marvel at what strange coincidence it was, but at that moment I had no idea who she was. I just thought she was a client or a prospect. The word urgent made me open it.

Without warning my safe little world with its little plan of illicit oral sex under Josh's desk crumbled into dust. My whole body went cold. I read the all-caps message in a state of blank shock.

HAVE YOU BEEN HAVING FUN FUCKING MY MAN?

GUESS WHAT, SLUT? I'M PREGNANT WITH JOSH'S BABY. WHY DON'T YOU GO FIND A MAN OF YOUR OWN, YOU NASTY PIG!!!!! GET SOME MORALS AND CLASS, SLUT. AND DON'T <u>EVER</u> TOUCH MY MAN AGAIN.

LILLIAN

The words swam before my shocked eyes. It had to be a joke. I wanted it so much to be someone's sick sense of humor. It just had to be, only it wasn't. I felt the venom of the words seeping through my skin, infecting my flesh and poisoning my blood.

Breathlessly, I stared at the scanned photo of an ultrasound. The mother's name was on the photo, too. Lillian Taylor. The photo was taken three days ago.

He had a girlfriend.

Oh shit. He had a fucking girlfriend.

A pregnant girlfriend.

I'd felt my world was falling apart around me twice before. When my parents announced their divorce and when Grandma died.

But this email… It was like a whole new level of world-shattering. I was in a threesome and I didn't even know it. I had somehow become the hated other woman. That creature that steals other women's men. Me? Just when I was thinking about taking things to the next level with Josh, I find out he's a fucking two-timing piece of shit.

I trusted him and he turned out to be no better than my slutty neighbor. Maybe even worse. At least that guy never let them expect anything more than a screaming orgasm. To think Josh had been lying to me all along hurt.

How could he have done what we did—lying in bed with me, kissing me, looking into my eyes and telling me how important I was becoming to him while he was having unprotected sex with a woman who sent out all-caps emails?
Thank God, we always used a condom.

I looked down at my hands. They were shaking. With anger. The liar. He was such a fucking liar. All those long lingering looks. There was no way I could sit at my desk for the rest of the day and pretend I didn't know about her when all I wanted to do was go up to him and throat-punch him. How dare he? How long had Lillian been in the picture? The fact that she knew about me and I didn't know about her, meant she'd been in the picture the whole time.

I lifted my head and looked around me. Everyone else had their heads down and seemed to be engrossed in their work. I needed to be professional about this. *Be cool, Mimi. You're not the first fool to get played. Be professional. No need to fuck up your career over a cheating prick.*

I took three deep breaths. I could be professional about this. I could play this game. Three calming breaths was obviously not enough because my blood was still boiling.

Alice popped her head around my cubicle.

I whipped my head around. "What?" I growled.

Her eyes widened. "Never mind," she muttered and slunk away.

I took another three breaths. *Calm down, Mimi. You worked long and hard at this job. You're going to be out of this cubicle and into your own glass office in a few months. Mustn't jeopardize that. Oh no, no, no. No fucking man was worth that.*

Three more extra-deep breaths.

But, nope. I couldn't be professional about it. I needed to talk to that lowlife or I would explode. I stood. My legs were shaking. Actually, everything shook. Even my insides. My stomach roiled.

I took another steadying breath.

He was definitely not worth losing my breakfast over. I paid good money for that egg white sandwich, and even if I was going to lose it, I want to lose it on his shirt-front. My head turned automatically in the direction of his office. He waved and winked at me.

Bastard. Cheating, lying bastard!

But I had more chutzpah in me than I realized: I waved back.

I picked up my cell phone from my bag, straightened my skirt, and with my head held up high, I walked past all the glass offices towards the restrooms. As I passed his office, I pretended I had just received a call and made out as if I was completely engrossed in my fake telephone conversation.

By the time I reached the washroom, my whole body was rigid with fury. Wow! I'd never been so spectacularly cheated on before. I stood in front of the mirror and looked at myself. How amazing to see that I looked so normal on the outside while inside I was churning so much I could start making butter. I called my best friend, Megan. She was always the first one I called whenever something great, bad, or in between happened. The girl could have been in the middle of the biggest deal of her life, but she would've dropped everything for me. And I'd do the same for her.

"I'm sorry to bother you at work," I said, "but everything just went to hell here."

"Why? What happened?" she asked in an urgent whisper. If she was whispering it meant other people were in the next room.
"Josh has a girlfriend and she's pregnant."

"What? The little snake," she shouted, then remembered

herself and dropped back down to a fierce whisper. "That two-timing, creepy jerk. I knew he was no good. How did you find out?" I heard her footsteps. She must be leaving her office and going out of earshot.

"She sent me an all-caps email, that's how," I replied, my voice shaking with shock.

"Oh. My. God. Forward it to me," she demanded in her normal voice.

"Megan?"

"What? I'd love to see what an email from a wronged girlfriend all in caps looks like."

"This is serious. I'm so angry I feel like killing him."

"Um…okay. What are you going to do?"

"Confront him."

"What? Like now?" she asks incredulously.

"No, next year. Of course, now."

"I think you better wait until after office hours, babe," she suggests seriously.

"I don't think I can last that long. I'll explode."

"Of course, you can wait. You need your job, Mimi. Fuck him. He doesn't deserve you and he's definitely not worth losing your job over."

"No, I'm going to confront that lying rat right now," I yelled

"No," she yelled right back. "If you do, things are going to get so uncomfortable you're just going to end up without a job."

"Whatever," I said.

"Don't do it,' she warned, but I rang off, and marched to Josh's office.

6

MIMI

He was alone. How many times had I looked through those glass walls and smiled at him? How many times had he smiled back when he felt my eyes on him? I used to fantasize about going in, locking the door behind me, pulling the blinds shut, and straddling him, right there in his chair. Or, maybe letting him take me on the desk. All sorts of things. Now I wanted to lock the door and kick his face in.

Feeling the weight of my stare, he looked up and smiled.

I closed the glass door behind me and locked it. "Funny thing," I said, as I walked over and started pulling the blinds closed. His eyes lit up. Ass wipe thought I was coming to give him a blowjob under the desk.

"Oh, come to Big Daddy," he smirked and I actually felt physically sick. Funny how I would have thought that was sexy at one time—maybe ten minutes earlier. Right now, letting me anywhere near his dick could result in serious, probably untreatable injury.

I wished I could hurt him as much as I was hurting just then. I swallowed hard. The fury was like a stone in my throat. "Maybe you should check with your girlfriend first."

"What?" he asked, and his voice must have risen an entire octave.

"Are you honestly gonna pretend you don't know who I mean? You're going to sit there, and act like I don't know what I'm talking about?"

He stood, hands out. "Mimi, is this a joke?"

"I haven't gotten to the funny part yet," I said. "I got an email from a woman who claims to be pregnant with your child."

His first reaction actually made me doubt myself. Either he was a damn good actor or Lillian Taylor was a wholesale liar. He looked at me as if I had turned into a giant scaly lizard. "What on God's sweet earth are you talking about?"

The sensation of hope that fluttered inside me was almost as strong as the sense of guilt. I hadn't given him a chance to defend himself. She could be some crazy lunatic. I didn't have a shred of proof other than a stupid scan with her name on it. That proved nothing. What if I had jumped to the wrong conclusion?

With much less certainty than I had come into the room with, I walked up to him and showed him my phone.

He gasped. Unlike his original fake surprise, I believed this expression of shock.

"She's pregnant?" He stared up at me his eyes wide and shining. "Hell, who knew? I'm shooting live rounds. Why didn't she tell me?" he crowed. There was a strange mixture of joy, hope, and exasperation in his voice. It told me everything I needed to know.

I felt as if I was in an alternate reality. I wanted to break something. Preferably, his legs. Or neck. Or at the very least, bash his head in with the spiky end of my shoe. Multiple times. I'd probably ruin it, but it would be worth it if I could see his brain flow out.

"So, you *are* seeing someone else," I said through clenched teeth.

He looked distractedly at the phone sitting on his table before dragging his eyes back to me. The fucking bastard couldn't wait to call her!

"Look," he cajoled. "I never said we were exclusive."

My gut burned. "What?"

He shrugged. "Come on, Mimi. You're a grown woman. I thought you knew we were just messing about."

I took a step back and stared at him with hatred. "You told me I was special."

"You are special."

"To you," I reminded.

"Well, it was a heat of the moment thing."

"You *told* me you were single."

He shifted uncomfortably. "Well, technically I am single."

I shook my head incredulously. "I don't believe this."

He looked at me with bovine stupidity. "Come on, Mimi. None of this needs to get awkward. We just lived a little."

"Lived a little?" I exploded. "I can't believe you could be so callous. How could you lie like that?"

I might as well have been talking to myself. From the moment I mentioned his fetus, everything else went out the window. He ran his hands through his short, curly brown hair—hair I'd tangled in my fingers—and hit his chair with a soft thump when he fell into it. His eyes darted back and forth.

"Hello?" I waved my arms back and forth furiously.

"Oh, yeah. Um. I'm sorry…but this has really thrown me." He laughed nervously, clearly in shock. He didn't care about me at all and never would.

I watched him make an effort to placate me. "We had some fun. Let's just put it behind us and… um… go back to what things were like before any of this happened. We're a good team and there's no need to spoil that. Obviously, I'm really sorry if I hurt your feelings."

I hated it when someone used the word 'if' and 'hurt your feelings' in the same sentence. What the fuck? That means you don't even recognize that you did, but even if I didn't take that into consideration his little speech must have been the fakest, lamest, most insincere apology in the history of mankind.

How could I have been so blind not see what a slippery weasel he really was? At least weasels were cute. He wasn't even worth my anger. I straightened my spine and threw him a fake smile.

"Don't worry about it. I lied too. You know, that little problem of yours, the one that makes you eat pussy instead of fucking it, it's not normal, and you really should see a professional about it."

His eyes bulged as I smiled broadly and sailed out of the door with my head held high.

7

MIMI

J closed the door and raced to my cubicle. One of my other superiors jumped out of the way just in time to avoid getting run over. Great. Now, I'd have to explain why I was a total mess when I next saw him.

My hands were shaking with nerves, but I felt strangely victorious as I sank onto my chair. I had a ton of things I need to get through. There was a report that had to be in before lunchtime tomorrow and I was nowhere near ready to present it. I still had to attend the crappy status meeting at half-past twelve, but I didn't feel any pressure.

Instead, I knew I had to get out of the office. There was a cute little bar down the road. I should go and have a glass of something to settle my nerves. I picked up my purse. My cell phone rang.

"Have you done it?" Megan asked in an awed voice.

"Yes," I said coolly.

"What happened?" she whispered back. "Did you get fired?"

"No."

"Did you quit?"

"No, but I thought about it for a split second."

"Do we need to meet for lunch? Maybe a liquid lunch?"

"Hell, yes." I checked the time and told Megan I'd meet her at our favorite spot, situated halfway between our offices. Then I left my cubicle holding my stomach as I did. I made it a point to walk slowly past my direct boss's office.

"Mimi?" Tracee called.

I turned to look at her. "Yes?"

"Come in here, please."

I walked in with my hand still placed on my stomach.

"Are you all right?"

I shook my head, wincing as I did. "I'm not feeling very well," I whispered. "I thought I could push through and come in and be fine, but I think I ate something bad over the weekend."

"Oh, no. You should get out of here, just in case it's contagious." Bingo. The biggest germaphobe in the office. She even stood and increased the distance between us.

"If you can spare me, that would be amazing."

"Sure. You never call out. Go home, get some rest." I thanked her and walked out. I could see her rushing to open one of her drawers. Probably to disinfect herself. I didn't care. I shut down my laptop, got my things and hauled ass.

8
MIMI

"*He* said that?" Megan's mouth fell open. She was already holding a glass of wine since I'd ordered for her. I hadn't even waited for her to show up. I was on glass number two.

I nodded, my head resting on one hand. "He didn't even try to explain. I think he was too busy flipping out over the baby. You know?"

"That douchebag! What a complete fucking tool!" she ranted. Typical Megan, never pulling punches. Normally, I'd giggle and remind her we were in public, but I didn't care just then.

"How could I have let him trick me like that? I thought I was too smart to fall for a guy like him."

"Did you really fall for him?" she asked.

I saw sympathy written all over her face and felt a bit sorry for myself "I don't know. I thought I could have been, I guess. I thought we were about to take things to the next level."

"Oh, honey." She put a hand over mine. "I could fucking kill

28

that man for what he did to you." She raised her other hand and signaled for more drinks. I didn't bother to stop her. My work day was officially over, anyway.

"I wonder how the girlfriend found out about you?" she asked.

"I don't know and I don't care, but I'm glad she did. I am. I really am. It makes my skin crawl to think I was the other woman this whole time. I hate that I let him do that to me." I shivered at the thought.

"You'll get through this," she said, nodding her head so hard her springy red curls shook in every direction. "It's not your fault, either, so I won't hear any of that. You didn't walk into this meaning to hurt anybody. He lied to you. You thought you were starting something good. Nobody could blame you for that. Besides," she added with a wink, "being the other woman isn't the end of the world."

I blinked once, then twice. "Wait. What?"

"What?" she asked, shrugging.

"You were the other woman?"

"I thought you knew that story!" She took off her blazer, which was a clue that the story was going to be a good one, then pulled her curls into a loose twist. I settled in for the story, grateful for the excuse to stop thinking about my own misery.

"Okay. So, you remember my first boss at the ad agency?"

"The one who reminded you of Jon Hamm in *Mad Men*?" I rolled my eyes, remembering the hours I had to listen to her going on about what a genius he was and how incredibly lucky she was to have such a brilliant mentor. And, of course, all about what a gorgeous hunk of man he was. Then, I gasped. "Wait. Are you telling me you slept with him?"

She smirked.

"You didn't tell me!"

"I knew you'd get all judgy."

"I wouldn't have! I swear to God! Do you think I'm that sort of person?" I asked, aghast.

"Okay, so maybe I was projecting. I don't know. I think deep down I was feeling guilty. It wasn't a secret that he was married—his wife's picture was on his desk." She crinkled her nose. "I didn't mean for it to happen, but at the end of the day, I justified it to myself that I didn't owe her any loyalty. I didn't put the ring on her finger. If he wanted to cheat on her, it was between the two of them."

"But you always said sleeping with the boss was a disaster waiting to happen."

She took a sip of her wine. "It is. Why do you think I left?"

"Did she find out?"

"No idea. I knew I didn't want to do it anymore, and being in the same space as he was had become awkward. So, I left but the end wasn't pretty."

"I cannot believe you let five years pass without telling me this. What else have you been holding back?" I leaned forward, suddenly more interested in her life than I was in my own.

Her green eyes sparkled. "Wouldn't you like to know?"

"Yes. I would like to know. Which is why I'm asking."

"What about you?" she countered. "You always get all shaky and jumpy whenever I mention Rich's friend, Alex."

I felt my cheeks go red. "That was a long time ago."

"So, you did sleep with him, you little liar! I knew it!"

"I wasn't exactly proud of myself," I said, looking around as if anybody would care even if they overheard. The lunch crowd was heavy, but it seemed like everybody was too busy with their own lives to care about mine. That was one thing about living in the city: rarely, if ever, did people waste their time paying attention to what happened around them. There were just too many people, too many conversations.

"Gee, I can't imagine why. He was living on Rich's couch at the time. Oh, God, please tell me you didn't do it on the couch." When I squirmed, and looked at the floor, she squealed, waving her hands around. "Oh, gross, Mims!"

"We got caught up in the moment," I said, wincing.

"I used to hang out on that couch with Rich after Alex left," she said, groaning.

"Oh, please, tell me you guys didn't do it on there."

She squinted, wrinkling her nose. "Not after he moved out..."

"Ew! Before! I had sex where you had sex!"

She waved her hands frantically, grossed out. The glass of wine I had drunk took effect and we both dissolved into giggles.

She started her second glass of wine, raising it to me before taking a sip. "Remember Bradford?" She rolled her eyes, affecting a strong, WASP-y accent when she said his name.

"Oh, him. I tried to forget him. What a stuck-up prick."

"Remember that time you tried to call him Brad?" she giggled.

"Yeah, and then he launched into a twenty-minute monologue about the origin of his name and how it stretched back to the Revolution. Talk about insufferable. He's probably engaged to a girl named Angelina or Muffy or something."

"Muffy?" We both burst out laughing. I should have known then that it was time to slow down. It wasn't all that funny, but we leaned on each other and cracked up like it was.

"I think we should get something to eat," Megan suggested, wiping tears from her eyes. "I need to soak up all this wine."

"Agreed." We ordered a plate of French fry nachos, which was basically nothing more than nachos with fries in place of chips. A work of genius, in other words.

"Okay, I've gotta ask." She folded her arms on the table, leaning forward. "I know you don't wanna talk about it, but what are you going to do about your job after this?"

9

MIMI

"*I*'m not leaving, if that's what you're hinting at," I said fiercely.

"You're sure you can face him?"

"He's not my boss. It's a big department. I don't have to deal closely with him if I don't want to. I can still be professional."

She frowned. "Mimi. Not that you're immature or unprofessional, but you're going to need time to get over what happened."

"I'll be just fine. I refuse to let him ruin things for me. I've worked too damn hard to earn respect in that job, and I'm so close to that promotion." I sat back in my chair, swirling the Pinot Grigio in my glass. "I don't want him to win. He lied and cheated. I know he'll keep going on with his life like nothing happened between us. He's just that oblivious. So why should my career suffer if his doesn't?"

"Damn straight, girl." She clicked her glass against mine.

"Don't let him determine what happens with your life. You're the one in control. You call the shots."

"Why do I feel like I keep running up against the same issues over and over again?" I mused.

"What do you mean?"

"Between this and the bullshit with the buyer in my building."

"Oh, that." She waved a dismissive hand. "That doesn't mean anything."

"But it reminds me that there are people in the world who think they can do whatever they want. They can force people out of their homes, they can cheat on their girlfriend. Their pregnant girlfriend."

"Then again, there are people like you who are stronger and better than all that. You'll come out on top because it's where you belong."

"You're right."

She cupped a hand around her ear. "I'm sorry? I didn't hear you."

"You're right!"

"As always."

Our nachos came, and for a little while, there was nothing else in the world except for them. And more wine. Before I knew it, the lunch crowd was long gone and the Happy Hour crowd had started to trickle in. After we'd killed our nachos, we followed it with an order of chicken fingers. We'd also consumed enough wine to make the room spin.

"I guess I should've gone back to work," Megan muttered.

"One of the perks of being a manager," I grinned, leaning my head on my hand. Everything was awesome. I was in a great mood. I had the best friend in the world, I had a great apartment, I had a great life in the best city in the world. Life was beautiful from where I sat.

Then I stood up, and things got a lot less beautiful. I realized, dimly, somewhere in the teeny tiny corner of my mind where sobriety still existed, that I'd spent the entire afternoon sitting in one spot. I had no idea how drunk I was until I stood up. And then? Oh, boy.

"Shit, I'm wasted." I heard myself slurring. I told myself to stop slurring, which, of course, only made things worse.

"You want me to take a cab with you?" Megan asked.

"Nah. We're in opposite directions," I said, stumbling towards the door. I laughed at myself, then hated myself for laughing. I didn't like getting this drunk when I was out and about in the world. If I was at a friend's place and could crash, awesome. Otherwise, I tried to maintain a buzz. Then again, I didn't normally find out the guy I was ready to become exclusive with had just impregnated his girlfriend. It was a big day of firsts for me.

I managed to get my address right after falling into a cab, which as far as I was concerned was a good step in the right direction. The ride to my building was sort of a blur, during which I closed my eyes and leaned my forehead against the closed window. I already imagined calling out the next morning. It would have to be a long-lasting stomach bug. I'd probably sound like hell when I called Tracee, so that was a plus.

Only one problem. When I reached my front stoop and dug

through my purse for my keys, my hand touched nothing that resembled keys.

"What the hell?" I muttered, finally sitting down on the steps with my purse spread open. I used my phone's flashlight to get a better look. Drunkenly, I upended my purse. Huh. Wallet, makeup, tissue, mints.

Then I remembered putting my keys down on my desk that morning, having used the electronic fob on my keychain to get into the building. And I'd never picked them back up.

"Shit! What an idiot?" I cursed my head in my hands. "Damn and hell!" What did I do now? I was wasted on my front stoop with no way to get into my apartment.

MIMI

*S*itting on the front stoop, feeling drunker than I'd been in a very long time, I hazily tried to think of what to do. I couldn't even get through the entrance door without my key, much less my apartment. The idea of climbing up the fire escape and trying my bedroom window occurred to me, but even I wasn't drunk enough to think that might be a good idea in my condition. I wasn't the most coordinated person while sober.

This was probably the worst day of my life in years, and it was only getting worse. I was dangerously close to crossing the line from fun drunk into depressed drunk—actually, no, I was actively stepping over the line at that point.

I leaned against the stone banister with a sigh. Why me?

Should I call Megan and ask to crash with her? I dreaded the thought of the cab journey all the way to her place. I should call the building supervisor, I decided. Only I couldn't remember his number and wasn't sure I could make sense of my contact list just then. I was sure the Universe was watching me as the subject of an intergalactic prank show. My episode had finally come up.

"Hello?"

I opened my eyes, squinting to focus on the figure standing at the foot of the steps. When he came into focus, my stomach sank. Yep. A bunch of unseen beings were laughing their butts off at me just then. Because it was him. My neighbor. Mr. My Shit Doesn't Stink.

Of course, he looked just as yummy as he had that morning, only he'd lost the tie at some point. His shirt was open at the collar—in other words, just when I thought he couldn't get more ridiculously handsome, he showed me how little I knew.

"Hello," I said, sitting up and gathering my dignity.

He looked back and forth, then up at me. "Do you need help with something?"

"Does it look like I need help?"

"Are you really asking me that question?" I thought I saw a smile on his face. I knew I heard it in his voice. Still, I couldn't tell if he was laughing at me to be mean, or just because I looked like a hot mess. He hadn't exactly proven himself to be a nice guy up to that point.

"I thought I would sit outside for a while," I explained.

"To clear your head a little? It usually helps me after I've had too much to drink."

"Wow," I said, eyes wide. "Judgmental much?"

"Excuse me?"

"You just assumed I've had too much to drink."

38

"It wasn't an assumption. You're slurring all over the place."

"I'm not slurring. I'm talking in cursive."

"I can smell the alcohol from up here."

"You so cannot." I held a hand in front of my mouth and breathed on it, then breathed in. "Yep. You probably can."

"And I'm not judging. I've seen some pretty wasted chicks in my time, and you don't even rank."

"Oh, I'm sure you have," I said, rolling my eyes. I leaned against the banister again, deciding what the hell. He knew I was drunk. I didn't care anymore.

"Haven't you?" He started up the steps, slowly. "It's New York. All you have to do is hang out in front of a club on a Saturday night. Any club." He sat down beside me, forearms on his knees. "I'd give you a hundred bucks for every girl who walks out with her shoes on her feet instead of in her hands."

I didn't mean to laugh. I didn't want to give him the satisfaction. But I did, snorting loudly for good measure. That made him laugh, too. He had a nice laugh. It made my toes curl.

"I'll have to take you up on that," I said.

"You should. I don't expect to lose much money." He looked around again. "So, you're locked out?"

I nodded. "I left my keys at work."

"And then you sucked down a few bottles of wine."

I lifted my forefinger and pointed it at him. "That sounds pretty judgmental for a person who's not judging me."

"But it's also probably a fact." He slid a sleek phone from his pants pocket. "I'll call the Super for you."

"You will?" I couldn't have explained why that touched me the way it did, but I felt all fluttery at the offer. There are some kind people left in the world.

"No problem." He looked over at me. "By the way, I'm Max."

Max, short for Maximus. "I'm Mimi Young"

He reached the Super. I listened to him ask him to come by. Then he nodded a few times and hung up. "Mimi Young, this is not your night. I'm sorry to tell you that."

I groaned, throwing my head back. "Why?"

"Because the Super's at his kid's school show, and it doesn't let out until ten." Max shook his head, then muttered, "I really didn't need his whole life story."

"Three hours?"

"It's a good sign that you can still do basic math."

"Ugh." I couldn't believe my luck. I truly couldn't.

"No chance in getting back to work to pick up the keys, huh?"

I frowned as I thought about it. My passkey was on that keychain and the building was completely secure at night. "No. Like the guard wouldn't even let me in without it."

Max blew out a long breath. "Well, there's only one thing to do."

"What?"

"You can wait in my place if you want. It's only three hours. Not a tragedy."

I side-eyed him. "You don't have anything better to do?"

"Would I offer if I had anything better to do?"

"So, if you had something better to do you would leave me sitting out here."

He smirked. "Probably. Come on."

I was determined to stand on my own since I still had a modicum of dignity left, or so I told myself. What I did not have, I soon found out, was coordination. I couldn't seem to make my legs work. I heard him sigh, then felt his hands grip my biceps as he lifted me up. The fact that he could do that so easily was not lost on me.

When we got in the elevator, I leaned against the wall and watched him openly. In the light, he looked even better than he had in the dark.

"What?" he asked, looking down at me out of the corner of his eye. He had at least a half-foot on me even though I was in heels.

"Do you think it's weird? Like, does it ever feel weird to you?"

"Does what feel weird?"

"Living as one of only two people in our whole building?"

He waited a moment, then nodded. "Not really."

"You won't cave in to those bastards, will you? They can buy everybody else out, but they can't buy us. We'll stand our ground and fight them until the very end," I declared dramatically.

He stared at me. "To the very end," he agreed softly.

"I woke up this morning and felt like I was in one of those disaster movies where only a few people are left."

"Like *The Stand*."

"Oh, that movie was awful."

"Terrible," he agreed. "The book was much better."

"But you see what I mean."

"I do." He grinned. "Well, at least you're not totally alone. Otherwise, you'd still be sitting out there on the steps."

"You don't know that. I might know people in the neighborhood."

The doors opened, and Max stepped out with a knowing grin. "Who?"

"Joe."

"Joe who? And don't say Smith."

"I wasn't going to." I put all my effort into walking a straight line as we made our way down the hall."

"So, you don't know anybody in the neighborhood. Just admit it. It's not a crime. This is New York. It would be weird if you did."

"Okay, I don't." I leaned against the wall while Max unlocked the door.

He grinned. "So, I'm kind of your savior right now?"

"I could just as easily sit out in front of my door for the next three hours."

He stopped just short of opening his door. "You're right. See ya."

"No, no. Come on. I was just kidding."

He smiled—he had a really, really nice smile, when he bothered to show it off—and opened the door.

"Whoa." I dropped my purse just inside the door, stunned at what I saw. "This is waaaaaay bigger than my place! How many bedrooms is this?"

"Um, three?"

"Wow. Your living room is twice the size of mine. Maybe three times." I walked around, running my hands over the furniture. All new, all very nice. Mine was from Ikea or Goodwill. His had actually come from a furniture store, and it actually matched. "And your view!"

"Yeah, it's pretty nice."

"My view is of the back alley. This is better than nice." I could see the entire street out his living room windows, not to mention the city skyline over the tops of the roofs across the street. "This is fantastic. I can see why you don't want to leave. I wouldn't, either."

"It's nice," he said again. "I like the area." He paused then added meaningfully. "And the scenery."

His comment flew over my head for a second as I stood by the window, but as the meaning of his words sank in, I felt my cheeks redden.

"Then how come you've never been very nice to me when I've run into you before?" I asked, turning halfway.

He slid out of his suit jacket, folding it carelessly over the back of a leather club chair. I could make out the size of his shoulders and biceps through the cut of his white shirt. My stomach fluttered a little—maybe not a good thing, considering the amount of food and booze in there. I'd always been a girl who loved a solid set of shoulders, and his were impressive. Much like the rest of him, come to think of it.

"I'm not always great with strangers," he admitted. "And I'm usually lost in my own head when I'm alone."

"I don't understand."

He grinned, shaking his head. "I mean I'm usually distracted. I have a million things going on in my head all the time. That's all. People take that as rudeness when I'm just…oblivious, I guess. Not something I'm proud of."

I looked him up and down, trying to decide if he was sincere or not. Then I gave up since I was no judge of character in my condition, and his smile and dimples were too distracting.

"You want something to drink?" he asked.

I brightened. "You have any wine?"

"Yeah, but I was thinking water might be a better idea right now. No offense, but I like my furniture puke-free."

I was just about to protest when a nasty belch worked its way up my esophagus. *Oh, sexy,* I thought in panic. I managed to keep my mouth closed, turning my head away from where he stood. "Yeah," I agreed when it had passed. "Water's great."

I watched as he walked into the open kitchen, which also

happened to be three times larger than mine. It was very sleek, all black and chrome. Very masculine. I wondered how much work he'd had done in there. I would have asked, only the sight of his tight butt was more interesting just then. He was bent and pulling two bottles of water from a low shelf in his fridge.

I suddenly hoped the Super took all night to get here.

MIMI

"Come. Sit." Max sat on the black leather sofa, then patted the spot beside him. "Take a load off. I'm sure your feet are killing you in those things."

I looked down at my heels. "These? They're probably my most comfortable shoes."

"Impossible."

"Not impossible. Believe me, I have way less comfortable ones than these."

"Now it sounds like you're bragging." He crossed one ankle over the other knee, looking completely relaxed yet panty-meltingly hot at the same time. If the bottle of water in one hand had been a martini, he could've passed for James Bond. He was just so overwhelmingly marvelous.

"I'm not bragging. I'm just saying." I sank gratefully into the buttery soft leather. "Oh, my. This is very, very comfortable," I gushed.

His eyes crinkled. "Yeah, it's comfortable."

I pointed to the massive flat screen that took up most of the opposite wall. "How much does something like that cost?"

"Do you always ask the price of things when you visit somebody's apartment for the first time?"

"No, but I do babble incessantly."

"Gotcha." He looked at the TV. "It was a gift, actually."

"A gift?" I blinked. "Who the hell gives gifts like that?"

"A client of mine."

I looked at the TV, where we were both reflected. "Is your client a King? An Arab Prince? A Mexican drug lord?"

He threw his wonderful head back and laughed. He had a great laugh, deep and resonant. "No. He's even wealthier than that, actually."

"Not to brag or anything," I shot back but messed it up with a stupid giggle. I had to stop myself, but it was as if my mouth had a mind of its own.

He looked at me seriously. "No, not at all. It's a fact. He is."

I tilted my head to the side, seeing him through new eyes. "What do you do?"

"I work with rich people." He raised the water bottle to his lips. The end of that part of our conversation, obviously. Just as well, since I couldn't think straight while I was sitting so close to him. He had this intense masculinity that I just couldn't resist. I crossed my legs in his direction.

"So, Max. What should we do to pass the time until the Super gets here?"

He looked over at me out of the corner of his eye, and I

wasn't sure whether I saw a knowing smirk play along the corners of his mouth. "Gee, I don't know. What do you think we should do?"

Shoot. I didn't expect him to lob the ball back in my direction like that. I had no follow-up line. Boy, was I rusty with flirting. I tried to remember how Josh and I originally started out together.

Josh. It all came rushing back at once. My chin trembled before I could stop it.

"Um… Are you okay?" Max looked alarmed.

"Sure, I'm fine." Only the word "fine" came out in a loud, bleating sob. The dam broke, and all the pent-up pain and disappointment of the day came pouring out of me.

"Jesus," I heard him say. "What happened?" He handed me a box of tissues. I tried to thank him, but I was crying too hard.

"My…boyfriend…my…ex-boyfriend," I said bitterly.

"Ohhhh. Is that why you went out and got ripped up?"

I nodded, then blew my nose. It sounded like a cross between a tugboat and a trumpet. So hot. Who wouldn't want a piece of me just then? "He…we were dating for over a month. I thought he was going to take it to the next level," I sniffed pitifully.

"That sucks."

"You don't even know the half of it." I let out a wail. I didn't even care anymore that I sounded like an idiot. I'd gotten started, and there was no stopping me.

"What's the rest of it?" he asked. I felt his hand on my back. He didn't rub, he didn't pat. He just placed his large warm hand on my back. Somehow, that was enough. It was quite lovely, actually.

"He has a girlfriend!"

"Oh, the bastard."

"And she's pregnant."

"Whoa."

I nodded empathically. "She emailed me at work, called me out, and sent me a picture of the ultrasound of her baby. I still can't believe I never once suspected that I was the other woman," I wailed inconsolably and leaned my forehead on his shoulder

"It's not your fault, Mimi," he soothed.

I wasn't looking up, and even if I was I wouldn't be able to see through the tears in my eyes, but it was so great being so close to him I could have stayed there forever.

"You didn't do anything wrong."

"I didn't tell you the worst part," I hiccupped.

"Don't tell me you're pregnant too."

I gasped. "Oh, God, no!"

"Then it's not that bad."

"He's my boss."

"Oh, God."

I nodded and sniffed. "He's not my boss, but he's a manager and I have to see him every day. I just hate it that I got involved with somebody at work because only stupid people do that." I looked up at Max through a veil of tears. "I'm not a stupid person. I swear, I'm not stupid. You have to believe me. I'm holding my heart in my hands."

"I believe you." His smile was kind, even sweet.

I wiped my eyes. It felt like the worst was over, which was a relief.

"Feel a bit better?"

"No fair," I muttered to myself.

"What's no fair?" he asked.

"You don't get to be so gorgeous and be a nice guy, too."

"Gorgeous?" He had been leaning in, close to me, but straightened away. "I wouldn't call myself gorgeous."

"Oh, come on," I cried indignantly. "Is your mirror broken? Or do you have really poor eyesight? Is that it?"

He chuckled. The sound caused another strange flutter in my stomach. I looked at him. "My stomach is fluttering."

"You're not going to be sick, are you?" he asked anxiously.

I couldn't believe he could make me laugh when I felt so completely crushed, but he did. I tried to hold it in, but before I knew it I was laughing like a hyena. Couldn't stop. He just stared at me.

"Ugh. I'm the worst." I held my head in my hands. "I'm so that girl right now."

"That girl? What girl?" His hand was on my back again. He rubbed back and forth—not sexily, not like he was coming on to me. Just in a friendly sort of way. It was sort of amazing, though.

"The one who makes bad decisions. She gets sloppy drunk and does stupid things like go to a stranger's apartment and cry her eyes out like an idiot and tell him all her embarrassing issues. What a loser."

"Hmm. Would it make you feel better if I told you something embarrassing about myself?"

I looked at him through my spread fingers. "Oh, please. Like you have any embarrassing stories."

He grimaced. "I'm a human being. We all have embarrassing stories."

"Well, then, yes." I sat up, pushing my hair back over my shoulders sloppily. "Please. Soothe me with your embarrassment."

"Uh, let's see. When I was a kid, I played indoor soccer for maybe two seasons. I wasn't totally athletic back then. I was sort of a nerd."

"Bull...shit," I slurred. No way, was this guy ever a nerd. Not even in a past life. I felt quite aggressive about the fact.

"I was. I could show you some pretty tragic school pictures from those days."

"I will hold you to that."

"Anyway," he continued, "I had never scored a goal before, and suddenly the ball came my way. I was so excited because the goal was open, so I kicked it in. I thought I was a living god, you know? I mean cheering, waving my arms around, the whole thing. Only nobody else on my team was cheering."

I gasped and covered my mouth with my hands. "Oh, no. It was your goal, wasn't it?"

He nodded, rubbing a hand over his face. "Yeah. I scored on my own goal. It took years to live that one down."

I leaned my head back dreamily. "I can imagine. That's a pretty embarrassing thing to do."

"Believe me now that I was a nerd?" He said with a laugh.

"You were a nerd," I agreed slowly, even though secretly, he was even more of a sex god in my mind now that he had turned out to be totally the opposite of what I had expected. There was nothing sexier than a man who could laugh at himself. He put me at ease, he did his best to make me feel better. And he looked good enough to eat, on top of everything else.

"You should probably move your bed," I said suddenly.

"What?'

"I can hear you having sex," I stage whispered.

His eyes grew to twice their size. Up close his eyelashes were longer than a camel's.

"The headboard makes an awful racket," I added.

He folds his arms over his chest, his eyes alive with amusement. "Is the noise keeping you awake?"

"Nope. I use ear plugs, but once a picture fell off the wall, and hit me on the head," I said coolly.

His lips curved into a slow sexy smile. It was like watching a speeded-up video of a flower blooming. I couldn't look away.

MIMI

*M*aybe it was the wine. Maybe it was all the emotion—feeling bruised, vulnerable, taken advantage of, or maybe it was just that languorous smile. It made my teeth ache with lust. No matter the reason, I leaned in and kissed him before I could think twice about it.

"*Mmph!*" I took him by surprise, clearly, and he tensed at my sudden move, but that only lasted a split second. Suddenly he was kissing me back, and I was holding his stubble-roughened cheeks between my palms. His lips were so soft and strong at the same time.

His arms slid around my waist and tightened, and I let him pull me in. His tongue darted over my lips. I opened them, groaning as he explored my mouth. He sucked my bottom lip into his mouth and bit it. I gasped, and suddenly the kiss changed. It was no longer exploring but taking. My mouth was crushed possessively. I was stunned. Letting go of his face, my hands roamed over his powerful shoulders and the steely muscles of his arms, my brain exploding in pleasure and awe at his body.

I had never been kissed like this.

Something inside me snapped, and I lost control. My breath came out in a hiss, and he thrust his tongue into my mouth. I sucked it mindlessly. This was what I wanted all along. Scrambling into his lap, I straddled him and wrapped my arms around his neck. He went with it, running his hands over my back, my butt. I moaned, thrusting my tongue into his mouth.

We both panted, grunting, desperate.

I scooted closer and felt his thick hardness rubbing me between my legs where I throbbed for him. I rocked my hips against him. The lust was incredible. It was a thing that had a mind of its own. It made my head sing and my blood roar in my ears.

He groaned, gripping the back of my head with one hand, digging his fingers into my hair as he held me still. He drew my bottom lip between his and sucked before biting, gently, making me draw breath in a long hissing sound. The motion of my hips never stopped—if anything, my rocking sped up as the ache between my thighs grew more urgent. His free hand slid under my skirt, cupping my butt. I moaned, throwing my head back, ready to lose myself in him.

The ring of the doorbell shocked us both out of it.

I heard a voice on the other side of the door. "Hello?" The bell rang again. "Super!"

"You've gotta be kidding me," Max muttered.

I scrambled off his lap, suddenly mortified. Whatever happened to three hours? Meanwhile, he stood, making a quick adjustment below the belt before opening the door.

"Thanks a lot," I heard him say. "It means a lot that you came out so soon." I turned my face away so the man in the hall didn't see how hot and bothered I was.

"No problem," he said to Max. "My kid ended up getting stage fright, so we left early. Have a good one." I heard him walk away as Max closed the door.

I wanted to die. What the hell was I thinking, humping a total stranger? A nice stranger. A hot stranger. But a stranger I had to share a floor with. Why hadn't I learned my lessons the first time? Now I would have to avoid Josh at work and Max at home.

"Your key," he murmured. I held my hand out, still averting my eyes, and felt the cool metal touch my palm. My whole body was burning up so much I felt like a pork chop on somebody's barbecue.

"I should go," I whispered, gathering up my used tissues and purse and making a quick exit.

"Hang on," Max said, but I ignored him and rushed out.

When I got through my front door, I locked the door behind me. I didn't think. I just headed straight for the bedroom, threw myself on the bed and promptly passed out.

"*T*hat was totally unexpected," I murmured to myself, as I stared at the closed door.

The heat of her body was gone, but I could still taste the sweetness of her lips on my tongue. Her smell lingered on my shirt, flooding my senses. My cock was rock hard and aching, and my whole body burned with a raw need to slide my hand under her skirt and touch her smooth skin again. The urge to follow her to her place and finish what she started was shocking.

Wait a second…what the hell was I thinking?

The last thing in the world I needed was to fuck my neighbor. Dear God, imagine that kind of complication. No, just no. Even the idea should give me the creeps. My style was hit and run.

My antenna went up from the first moment I saw her a year ago. I knew she was trouble, and that was why I gave her a wide berth. I just didn't know how much trouble until a few minutes ago. Damn it to hell. Why did she have to lock herself out tonight?

I exhaled. What I needed was a stiff drink.

My favorite bottle of Scotch waited on the bar cart. The first sip helped me to herd my primitive thoughts back to reality.

There was no room for relationships or commitments in my life right now. I needed to focus on business. A woman like that would be pure distraction. The kind of distraction that could drive a man crazy. I had enough on my plate. The line had to be drawn right now. She was off limits. Absolutely, no more contact with her.

The second sip helped me remember I was living in a city with an endless supply of willing women. So, she was sexy and maddeningly cute with the goddamn most beautiful blue eyes I'd ever seen, but she was not irreplaceable. No one was. What I needed was more women like the one I had last night. Women who didn't make me want more than just one night with them.

I wondered uncomfortably what made me tell her about the soccer game. I'd never told anyone that story. She must be the sort of person who effortlessly tricked you into opening up and spilling cringeworthy memories.

All I had to do was keep away from her. She wouldn't be here long. She was fighting a losing battle. I knew how these things worked. The offers were going to get crazier and crazier, and one day her magic number would come up, and she would be gone just like the rest of the people in the building. It was only a matter of time. Once she was gone I'd never see her again.

My phone buzzed. I pulled it out and frowned when I saw who it was. Rule Number One: Never give your phone number to random hook-ups. Bridget was too foxy for that though. She knew my family so she hunted my mother down and tricked her with the "I left my Grandmother's earrings at his place" story. My unsuspecting mother gave her my number. Rule Number Two: Do not sleep with people who know your family.

"Hi, Bridget."

"Hi!" she squealed enthusiastically. That took care of my erection. Thanks, Bridget.

"I'm busy," I said, looking around my empty apartment. "Do you need something?"

She didn't even pause. "You. I need you," she purred.

I died a little inside. We'd had fun. Why did there have to be more than that? "I don't want to be a dick, Bridget, but we've had this talk before."

"I know, but there's nothing saying we can't have fun again, is there?" Her voice was low. She thought she was being seductive. If she knew how many times I'd heard that line, she'd cry herself to sleep.

"Actually, yes, there is. It won't be fun for me."

"Oh! Stop being so mean, Maximus." I hate women who call me Maximus. I could imagine her sitting in her apartment on the other side of town, pouting while twirling a lock of her blonde hair around one finger, trying to figure out how to trap me.

"I don't want to be an asshole, but you keep putting me in a position where I have to be."

"Don't get mad at me." Her voice broke on a sob.

Oh, for fuck's sake. Women. They were all fucking nuts. I took a deep breath. "I'm not mad," I said as calmly as I could. "You're a beautiful girl. You have a lot to offer. There's gotta be a lot of guys out there who would be thrilled to have you."

I poured a second drink. It was just that kind of night.

"But I want you, Max. You're the only guy who ever made me come like that." She gave a girlish giggle.

I smelled bullshit but kept my thoughts to myself. "That's a nice compliment." I walked to the bedroom, drink in hand, sat on the bed and took off my shoes. I was supposed to meet up with friends for dinner, but I missed it while waiting for the Super to get here. I guess I was in for the night—the way my luck was running, I'd end up getting an anvil dropped on me.

"It's the truth," she insisted.

"I believe you," I lied, putting my shoes away. I liked order, tidiness. In all areas of my life.

"So, why do you keep pushing me away?"

I really didn't need this hassle. I made a mental note to remind my naïve mother never to give my phone number to any woman again even if they claimed to have left their entire jewelry collection in my bedroom.

"I'm not pushing you away. I'm just letting you know again how it is. I enjoyed my time with you, but as I told you before, I'm not in the market for anything but casual sex," I said wearily.

"I was just hoping you would change your mind, I guess."

"I'm sorry, Bridget."

"Just give me a chance?" She needn't have bothered. She didn't have a chance in hell. The term one-timer was invented for women like her. She was jealous, clingy, needy, and stupid. Now, the sex-bomb next door. She was a whole different story. That's the kind of women you want to make memories with. Christ, I need to stop thinking about her.

"Look-," I began.

"Please," she begged.

I felt like an ass, and I didn't like feeling like an ass. No, it wasn't my fault she couldn't let it go. Damn my mother and her bleeding heart. "You should consider yourself lucky that you're not in a relationship with me. I'm a dick. I'm always working. I don't remember birthdays or anniversaries. I even forgot Christmas last year."

"I'm sorry for you," she blurted out.

"What?" I almost dropped my drink on the floor.

"I said, I'm sorry for you," she yelled furiously. For the first time since I met her, she sounded like a real person instead of a wannabe Marilyn Monroe. "I'm a nice person, and I have a lot to offer, but you won't let me into your life. I bet you meet a lot of nice girls. You've, um, met at least two of my friends. And that's just recently."

I grimaced. Women talked too much.

"You have all these bullshit excuses for why all you can do is hook up and move on. You'll never know what a good person I am."

I got undressed. "I really am very busy."

"Oh, I know you're very busy. You're a big deal." The sarcasm dripped from her voice.

This was getting boring. I would give one last try for our families' sake. "You wouldn't be happy with me, Bridget. I wasn't kidding when I said that. It's not just a line."

"You can't be happy, either. Nobody's happy when the closest relationship in their life is with their assistant."

"Right well. Thanks for calling." I had to hang up then, or else I would have said something to really piss her off. "Sorry, mother," I muttered and blocked her number.

I walked back into the sitting room and dropped down on the sofa. I picked up the remote and thought of Mimi asking me how much the TV cost and grinned to myself.

It was strange sitting there alone when I knew she was on the other side of the floor. All I had to do was go over there and knock on the door and I could have her. Then again, there was a good chance she was puking her guts up by now. Not sexy.

I thought about the jackass who'd cheated on her. She didn't know it, but that was a lucky escape. I raised my glass in a silent toast to the chicken shit, whoever he was for dropping her. He deserved to be tied down with a screaming brat. Idiot.

I watched some TV, but I was distracted. I couldn't stop thinking about the chick next door. How unfortunate that she was my neighbor. Restless, I roamed my apartment. I even thought about visiting my favorite lounge, I didn't have the heart to get dressed and go out again. Finally, I decided to turn in early. Definitely not the way I usually spent a Monday, or any night.

As I leaned over in my king size bed to turn off the bedside lamp, something funny happened. I remembered that only a wall separated me from the beauty next door and it gave me an instant erection. Her mouth was so soft and voluptuous. And that amazing ass. Round and full and…

Stop it, Max. Stop it.

I was wired and wide awake. I closed my eyes and forced myself to think of something else. With any luck, I wouldn't see her again.

*M*y first conscious thought on waking was the most fervent wish that I could just die and get it over with. My head was throbbing like there was a woodpecker in it. I hadn't even opened my eyes yet, but it already felt like the rays of sunshine coming through my bedroom window were trying to kill me. Why the hell hadn't I closed the blinds? Why was drunk me so stupid?

I pulled the blanket over my head, but that wasn't helpful since it meant having to smell my own breath, which was rank. I vaguely remembered throwing up twice during the night, and not having the will to brush my teeth. I made an opening for my breath to escape, hoping I'd at least reached the bathroom both times. I thought I had, but who knew? Maybe drunk me had decided to leave a surprise for poor, hungover me.

That was bad until I remembered my trip to Max's apartment. A whole other level of pain hit me.

"No. No. No," I groaned, whimpering a little from the pain in my head and in my heart. What was I thinking? Oh, right. I was thinking how hot he was, and how much I hated Josh.

What must he think of me? I could only imagine. Little snippets of our conversation came back making me cringe with shame. I was such a mess the entire time. Thank God, the Super had come when he did, or who knew where I'd be waking up—or where I would have thrown up. No way a make-out session like that one would have ended in anything but wild sex. I would have thrown up in his bed, on his body. Oh, God. It didn't bear thinking about.

I hated wine. I would never drink wine again. Wine was poor decision juice. Bad, bad wine.

No way I could make it to work, especially with the thought of seeing Josh. When I was free from the clutches of impending death, I would have to give a lot of thought to how to move forward. In the meantime, I fumbled around for my phone, grabbed it and pulled it under the blanket with me. Dialing Tracee, I left a mumbled message for her that included something about my stomach, feeling sick, and coming in tomorrow. The less detail, the better. Only people who were lying left lengthy messages.

I decided to venture out of bed a couple of hours later, after waking for the second time. I didn't feel much better, but I didn't feel any worse. It was a good first step. And no nasty surprises from drunk me. An excellent second step.

Once I got moving and decided my head was not, in fact, about to fall off, horror spread through me again as my behavior with Max last night worked its way into my thoughts again. I couldn't shake the memory of that...that kiss.

Actually, I don't even know if you can call what happened

just a kiss. Even in my state of total misery, the memory of the way his lips felt on mine was clear—and even a little bit of a turn-on.

I guess he had had a lot of practice. His technique was smooth, sexy, and so intensely masculine, he just about melted my panties clean off. I could imagine women throwing themselves at him. I didn't want to be just another one of those women. But I was.

Because if what I did wasn't throwing myself at him, I didn't know what was. I held my head in my hands, sitting on the edge of my tub as I waited for it to fill.

"I climbed onto his lap," I moaned to nobody in particular. "I tried to hump him. Oh, God."

But God wouldn't help me. God was too busy shaking His head in disappointment. It wasn't my fault. It was the wine's fault. And Josh's, since he was the reason wine and I got together in the first place.

As I soaked in silky bubbles, I imagined seeing Max again and barely managed to keep from drowning myself. No way. I couldn't put myself through that kind of humiliation.

"He probably thinks I'm a slut," I muttered miserably.

Well, his opinion is probably no better than it had been before. I vaguely remembered him giving some kind of explanation that he was lost in his own thoughts most of the time, but somehow, I didn't buy it. He was not lost in his thoughts. He was deliberately unfriendly to me, so it was not like I'd fallen far in his estimation. That was cold comfort, but it was the closest thing to comfort I had.

"Damn, Josh," I cursed aloud.

And I had ugly cried. Ugh! Stupid me. Then I remembered that Max had tried to comfort me. He had been nice, hadn't he? I wasn't misremembering it. At least, I didn't think so. I'd sure as hell never ask him face-to-face. There was only so much humiliation a girl could take.

I soaked in the tub until my skin pruned. By the time I got out, I felt a lot better—physically, at least. Mentally, on the other hand, all I could do was worry about what to say to Max when we ran into each other again. That was inevitable and I might as well prepare for it. I would thank him, of course, because he'd taken care of me. I owed him for that.

Maybe I could wear a bag over my head while I thanked him since I couldn't imagine looking him in the eye and I was sure my face would turn tomato red. Maybe a letter! That was it. I breathed a sigh of relief.

I would write a "thank you" letter. No, I would buy a card. And I'd thank him that way and slide it under his door. No. In his mailbox. That way, I wouldn't face humiliation if he happened to be on the other side of the door. Yes. Perfect solution.

When I walked out into the living room, my thoughts had moved from Max to the idea of breakfast. My stomach was still all sorts of messed up, thanks to the wine, but everybody who'd ever had a hangover knew that greasy food was the best solution. It didn't help that somebody nearby was cooking something that smelled incredible.

Then, I froze in place. Wait a minute. I didn't have any neighbors except for Max. No way could I smell cooking smells from other buildings. I tiptoed to the front door, sniffing the air. Sure enough, the smell got stronger the closer I got. What the heck?

I peered out the peephole, but the hallway was empty. Finally, I dared open the door, and what I found made my mouth drop open in surprise. On the floor, in a box, was a mouth-wateringly good hangover-breakfast-in-a bun that the Deli nearby specializes in, a liter bottle of water and a large cup of coffee.

I looked up and down the hall, but of course, Max was nowhere to be found. The big bun and the coffee were still hot, too. Hmmm...I wondered how he knew. My bath did make a horrible glugging sound whenever I unplugged it.

MIMI

The next day I bought a cute thank you card with a bashful bear holding a bunch of flowers on it and dropped it into his mailbox. I never heard or saw him. I was also gratified to note there were no more sexual noises coming from the other side of the wall. He had either moved his bed, or he hadn't brought anyone home. For reasons unknown, I found myself hoping it was the second option.

The first day back at work was the hardest, but I realized all I had to do to carry on as normal was keep away from Josh altogether. I found I had a great talent for it. In fact, it was quite amazing how many excuses I came up with to avoid him. I'd even started wearing headphones at my desk, just so the sound of his voice didn't turn my stomach. What a shame I couldn't get paid for avoiding Josh.

Incredible to think that there was a time when I was a master at inventing reasons to visit his office. How much effort I used to put into it. Dropping off papers, printing out reports rather than emailing them, even carrying random file folders into his lair just so I'd have an excuse if anybody saw me walking in.

Every time it had gotten to be a little much throughout the week, I'd remind myself that brunch at Megan's was only days away. It would just be the two of us and a couple of her friends from work. Nice girls who sort of drifted in and out of our weekly tradition depending on their plans. It was one of my constants, a way to decompress after a long week. And if there had ever been a long one, this was it.

I woke up on Saturday morning and felt pleased with myself. I had survived a whole working week and to be honest, it had not been too difficult. My work performance had not suffered either. In fact, Tracee had complimented me on one of my reports. In my mind, Josh had already become history.

Dressing in a white sweater, white jeans, and a dainty pair of pink butterfly sandals, I set off for the bakery around the corner from me.

"I'll have that coffee cake, please," I said, pointing to the last cake in the glass case. Thank God, I'd come in when I did because at least fifteen people had come up behind me to join the queue. No way would the bakery's legendary coffee not been snapped up by the time the line cleared up, not on a Saturday morning, anyway. I'd be the heroine of our brunch at Megan's.

I watched the girl behind the counter carefully put the cake into their distinctive purple box. A couple of moist, golden brown crumbs that were stuck to the utensil she used to move the cake dropped to the counter and lay there. Seductively. As if they were daring me to lick them off. This was cake porn at its finest. The girl, who was obviously a monster, wiped the lovely crumbs off with a dishcloth.

I transferred my lust to the cake in the box. It looked so good for a whole second I considered taking it home and having it all for myself. It would be worth the hours of toil at the gym as penance, not to mention Megan's disappointment. I watched the woman close the box and tie a purple ribbon around it.

Just then, as though Megan had read my mind, she texted me.

You'd better bring that coffee cake, lady. I swear I'll come around and search your apartment for it if you tell me they've run out.

Oh, well. There went that idea. I replied:

Got the last one! You may start raising money for the statue in my honor.

Carrying the bakery box by the ribbon, I elbowed my way to the door. Already, I was scanning the street for an available cab through the store's plate-glass windows. On a chilly Saturday morning, it usually wasn't easy to find one. We were in that time of year when nobody was quite used to the cooler temperatures yet and wanted to get into a warm car as quickly as possible. If we got to sixty degrees in January, on the other hand, the sidewalk would be thick with people jogging in t-shirts and shorts. Funny how that worked.

I looked down the length of the crowded street, hoping to spot a cab when my heart started fluttering. I recognized the dark hair, square jaw, and the broad shoulders. He seemed to leap out from the sea of mere mortals he walked among.

Oh shit!

I had, through a carefully thought-out schedule, managed to

avoid running into him at our building, but of course, I would have to meet him on the street with a million other people. Just my luck.

Still, there was no guarantee he had noticed me. I was one of dozens of people on the sidewalk. I decided to play it off like I hadn't noticed him as if I had way too many things on my mind to see him. Even if he was easily the most glorious thing in my line of sight. I kept walking, head held high as I scanned the street for a cab, still holding onto my coffee cake. Nobody could say my priorities weren't intact.

"Mimi!"

I froze in horror. That wasn't the voice I had expected to hear. All of a sudden, I realized Max was the least of my worries. I turned to find Josh striding toward me, an idiotic smile on his face. How could I ever have thought he was handsome? Oh, God, I actually slept with him. I needed to have my head examined.

With him was a tall glamazon of a woman, her face half-concealed by huge designer sunglasses. Her golden hair sparkled in the sun, and her clothing screamed 'I paid a small fortune for this'. She had one hand possessively curled round his arm. She could only be one person.

Unless I was willing to risk jumping into traffic as both Max and my ex along with his pregnant girlfriend, closed in on me from either side, there was just nowhere to run. My brain screamed in desperation.

"Mimi." Josh reached me, still smiling. To my shock and surprise, Lillian was smiling as well. Broadly too, I might add.

"Hi," I croaked. Why was she smiling? She thought I was a slut. The text of her email was burned into my poor brain forever. I'd never forget the feeling of her hatred coming through the screen at me. Yet there she was, beaming at me.

What if she was just trying to catch me off-guard? What if she took a swing at me? I couldn't hit a pregnant woman. Maybe I could offer her my coffee cake as a gesture of peace. No. Not the cake.

Josh put a hand on my arm. I told myself the burning sensation was just my imagination. The violent need to slap it off was not, though. I shook his hand off and took a step back.

"How are you? I've hardly seen you around the office these last few days," he boomed.

Are you insane? Are you literally crazy? Either that or it was me. I had dreamed the entire, crazy situation. How else could I explain away the warm, friendly, oblivious vibes I was picking up from the two of them?

"Listen," he continued, smiling adoringly at Lillian before turning back to me again. "You're one of the first to know. We got engaged and we're having our engagement party at the St. Regis in three weeks. You'd better be there." He laughed. "Or be square."

I blinked. What had I ever done to deserve this?

For her part, Lillian grinned like a cat that got the whole tub of cream and held up her left hand. Sure enough, there was a medium-sized diamond on her wiggling ring finger.

It was a nightmare. That was it. I was having a nightmare and in a few seconds, I'd look down and find out I wasn't wearing clothes. And everybody would point and laugh at me.

That had to be it. Nothing else made sense.

I was facing my ex and the woman he'd cheated on with me, and they were both smiling and inviting me to their goddamned engagement party. Why wouldn't I wake up already?

I opened my mouth to speak, but another voice cut me off.

"*W*e'd love to be there. Consider us a definite yes." With that, Max snaked an arm around my waist, pulled me tight against his body, and proceeded to crush my mouth in a long and passionate kiss. My knees went weak and I couldn't help my body from responding. Hormones were rushing around madly in my blood stream when he lifted his head and looked deep into my eyes. I stared back helplessly. After that lingering look, which I was completely unable to break, he turned to smile at Josh and Lillian.

I dared a look at Josh, my head still reeling from Max's sudden appearance and that kiss! I was glad for his arm around my waist, or I might have fallen to the ground. I was even quite shocked I had managed to hang on to the cake. The expression on my ex-boyfriend's face was priceless. If I had to describe it, "speechless shock and horror" would have been what I would have gone for.

"Uh…er…hi. Josh Williams." He held out his hand towards Max.

Max accepted it with a smile that reminded me of a shark. "Max Black." He looked down at me indulgently. "Is this the Josh from work you told me about?"

I wanted to kick him in the crotch, but I smiled, instead. "So, you do listen when I talk about work!"

I grinned at Lillian. "I don't know about you, but sometimes I feel like I'm talking to myself."

She didn't answer. She looked like she wasn't sure what was happening. She wasn't alone. I was still half-sure it was all a dream and I'd wake up sweating but relieved.

"Um, okay." Josh looked at me, then back at Max. The wind had definitely been taken out of his sails, I noticed with satisfaction. I could hear his brain work. Was she cheating on me?

I didn't dare let the smile slide from my face. "I'll see you at the office?"

"Yeah. Okay," he said but stood there like a dork.

"Well then. Thanks for the invite," I said into the awkward silence.

"See you there or be square," Max said for good measure. I nearly kicked him then.

Josh shook himself out of his trance and nodded. We both smiled and waved as my ex and his fiancée walked away. I managed to wait until they turned the corner before pushing Max's arm off me, then whirling around on him.

"Are you completely insane?" I hissed.

"Whoa! Calm down. Don't get your panties in a twist."

The cocky, arrogant SOB! "Calm down? Don't get my panties in a twist? Who the hell do you think you are?" I bellowed.

"You always this uptight?" His voice was mild.

"How dare you?" I gasped. I could feel my face getting red with anger.

"How dare I what?"

I looked at him with frustration. "Kiss me. Invite yourself to my boss's engagement party. Be a jerk."

He looked shocked, which only surprised me more. Was I supposed to be happy about that little display of his? He lifted his hands up. "Be a jerk? I was trying to help you."

I almost lost it. "Help me? That's my boss. I have to work with him," I growled.

"You said he wasn't your boss. He was just a manager." He looked over his shoulder, to where Josh had already disappeared. "And he looks like a real asshole."

"Well, thanks for the assessment," I said sarcastically, "but I have to coexist with him in the office."

"Yeah, and I just made it easier for you to do that," he reminded. "Unless you like knowing he thinks you're wasting away and still wishing the two of you were together."

"You don't know that," I said, rolling my eyes.

"I don't? What do you think that invitation was except for a way to rub it in your face? And don't kid yourself into thinking that fiancée of his wants you at her party except to make you feel like shit. I made it so you could at least show up, but you don't have to give her what she wants. I thought I was helping you save face," he explained. "I guess I was wrong."

I realized he was right, but all he had done was complicate matters. "I wish you would have let me know you were going to do that."

"I didn't know I was going to until I did. Besides," he added with a smirk, "you were acting like you didn't see me."

I tried not to look shifty. "Not true."

"True." He smiled, looking down at me with laughter in his eyes. He was amused. I amused him.

"I'm sort of in a hurry," I said, holding up the box with the coffee cake. "I'm meeting a friend for brunch. That's why I was a little distracted."

"Okay, okay. I'm not here to fight with you." He held up his hands, backing off. "Have fun at your brunch. And be sure to let me know what time I should pick you up for the party."

"What?"

"The engagement party." He turned and started walking away.

"Wait a minute!" I called out. "You don't really think we're going to that, do you?"

"Miss a party at the St. Regis? I'll even break out my good suit!" he called over one shoulder.

I marched after him, grabbed his hand, and pulled him around to face me. "Not so fast, Mister. I'm not going to that stupid party. First of all, I cannot imagine anything worse than spending an evening watching my ex and his new fiancé celebrate their great love for each other. He was out of order to even think of inviting me. Second, there's bound to be a bunch of people from work there, so I wouldn't dare go with a loose cannon like you. God knows what you could say or do. My job happens to be important to me."

"Not going would be a big mistake," he said slowly.

"Well, let me be the judge of that."

He shrugged. "Okay. It's your life. You're allowed to screw it up if you want to."

See, he didn't need to say that last part. He just did it to piss me off. I took a deep breath. "I don't want to sound ungrateful. So, thank you for helping me the other day, but from now on please do *not* help me. I do *not* need your help."

"100 bucks says you do!"

"Excuse me?"

He smirked and looked so damn sexy I wanted to bite him. "You heard."

"All right. You asked for it, buddy."

His expression lost that smug look. "What?"

"Five hundred bucks says you'll be needing my help before I need yours," I challenged. I knew I wouldn't need his help, but by chance, if he locked himself out of the building, needed to borrow sugar, or needed something, I could do with the money. I was lusting after a pair of shoes with a $465.00 sticker on it that I spotted in a shop window last week.

He chuckled, a twinkle in his eyes. "You're on."

"I'd like mine in fifty dollar bills, please," I said, with a glint in my eye. I'll show him.

His eyebrows rose mockingly, and I pretended to laugh.

Then he was gone, disappearing into the heavy Saturday morning crowd. And there I was, standing on the sidewalk with my heart banging, wanting him, and hating the fact that I wanted him.

19

MIMI

"*He* did what?" Megan screamed. She was sitting beside me on the sofa, her feet tucked underneath her.

I nodded. Thank heavens the other girls were running late, so I could run the whole terrible story past Megan in private. I sipped the Bloody Mary she'd handed me as soon as I arrived. She saw how stricken I looked and knew the very thing to make me feel better.

"I knew he was a spineless worm, but he's turning out to be a complete psychopath. You should be glad you're not with him. You don't want to be with someone like that. Are you glad it's all over?" she demanded.

I took a little sip of my drink. It was very good, actually. "I don't know! Jesus, it only happened on Monday!"

Her eyes became round. "You still want that jerk?"

"No, of course not. It's just the way he rushed out to get

engaged to her, and the way he acted just now like nothing had happened between us. It was like bizarro world. I guess it hurt me."

"They're both sick. That's the only way to describe it," she spat. She looked at me, all expectation. "So? What did you say?"

"I didn't say anything," I murmured, looking into my glass to avoid meeting her eyes. "Somebody else did the talking for me."

"Okay. Now you're starting to really intrigue me. Who did the talking?"

I laughed. "Don't freak out, but remember Max?"

I looked over to see her eyes get even wider and rounder than I'd ever seen them. "Your neighbor? Mr. You're So Fucking Big?"

I giggled. "Yeah. He saved me. I think." I gave her the details, watching as her jaw dropped further with each detail.

"He's your hero," she breathed, hands crossed over her chest.

"Oh, spare me. Since when are you such a romantic?"

"Since romantic things started happening in your life, Mimi Young!" She jumped up and down on the cushions, clapping her hands. Her silver bangles clashed musically.

"It's not romantic. It was just a coincidence that he happened to be there."

"You might try to sound convincing when you say things like that. I don't even think you believe it yourself, girl."

"I do believe it," I insisted firmly.

"You don't." She laughed. "You forget, I've known you since the first day of freshman year. I remember the shy little girl sitting on the edge of her bed in our dorm room. I know all about you, including all your tells."

"My tells?"

"What you do when you're lying," she said with a grin. "Even when you're only lying to yourself."

"What do I do?" I asked, suddenly curious.

"For one thing, you touch your ear. Left hand, left ear."

I dropped my hand to my lap. Megan threw her head back, laughing. "Next," she said once she'd calmed down, "your nostrils flare out."

"Oh, no." I pinched them closed.

"I'm just saying, you might want to think twice about spending money at the poker tables."

I sighed, chuckling in spite of myself. "All right," I murmured since it was just the two of us and she could read me so well, anyway. "There might have been a bit of drooling going on. I might have swooned a little."

"A little?" I was sure she was about ready to crawl out of her skin. "He's like a knight in shining armor. He keeps coming to your rescue."

"He was in the right place at the right time. He was probably chasing me down to embarrass me over Monday night, to tease me or whatever, and he over-heard what was going on. I told him about Josh, remember."

"Right, and he spared you the embarrassment of being in that situation alone. He's right—I bet that Lillian bitch told Josh to walk up and talk to you. I would bet anything she wanted to twist the knife in your chest."

"Yeah, well, the joke's on her. I don't know what I ever saw in him." I shook my head mournfully. "And she's marrying him! Shouldn't she know better? He won't change just because there's a ring on his finger."

"Who knows? Maybe she thinks she can change him." We both laughed, knowing that was impossible.

"Yeah, it's easier for her to blame me, even though I had no idea she existed until Monday."

"I guess she's pregnant and desperate," Megan conceded, jumping to her feet. Her long, loose caftan flowed, effort-lessly exuding style as she moved. At least I hadn't run into the Glamazon in my running clothes. I stood and followed her into the kitchen. It was a cramped little galley kitchen, just like mine, though hers was painted a sunny yellow to make up for the lack of windows.

"Well, at least now you don't need to worry about going to the party alone," Megan opening the fridge and took out a carton of tomato juice.

"I'm not going to the party at all."

"You have to go."

"No, I don't."

Megan calmly mixed another Bloody Mary for us. I made a mental note not to go overboard like I did on Monday. It was just not worth it. It took me two full days to recover.

"You have to go because if you don't. It means she wins. And you can't let her win. Do you want her to think she's intimidated you!? Believe me, if you don't show, that's exactly what she'll think."

I leaned against her counter. "I don't care what she thinks."

"If I were you, I'd go. Salvage my pride by showing up with an absolute hunk. From what you've told me, Max will do everything he can to make you look good."

She handed me a fresh Bloody Mary.

"Trust me," she said pouring herself one too. "My intuition is never off when it comes to things like this, and I think he's the real deal. He could have left you sitting there alone Monday night, but he brought you inside and tried to help when you lost your mind."

We clinked glasses. "Well," I said biting my thumb. "I told him I don't want him to go with me. I don't know what crazy stunt he'll pull next."

She took a sip. "Well, you'll just have to tell him, you've changed your mind."

"I can't do that."

"Why not?"

"Because we made a bet that he'd come to me for help before I went to him."

She grinned over the rim of her glass. "I think this could be the beginning of a very, very good romance novel."

"And I think you've already had too much to drink. No men for me in the immediate future. I need a break after Josh."

"Okay, then…" she trailed off, eyebrows arched.

The doorbell rang before I could ask what she looked so damn pleased with herself about.

20

MIMI

"*I*s everything all right with Josh?"

I turned in my chair on Monday morning to find Tracee standing in the doorway of my cubicle, but looking down the hall with a concerned frown. I stood, following her gaze. Josh's door was open, and the two of us watched him pacing back and forth like a maniac. He ran his hands through his hair, muttering something into his headset. He sounded extremely put out. I wondered who he was talking to.

"I don't know what's up with him, but if he keeps that up he'll have to replace the carpet," I muttered. "He's going to wear it down to the pad."

"He's been that way since last week," she said, shaking her head. "Like he's losing his mind."

I bit my tongue to keep from laughing. "It makes sense. I heard he got quite a surprise last week."

"Oh, of course. The baby. The engagement. I can't stand it

when men don't bother trying to leave their personal lives at home. If a woman came in here acting like a crazy person…"

"I know what you mean," I agreed.

She looked apologetic as she turned to me. "You know what's funny? This is going to sound crazy, but I sort of thought the two of you had something going on."

"Us?" I chuckled, even as my blood turned to ice.

"I know, it's crazy." She leaned in, winking. "You can do much better than him. I don't know what I was thinking. I hope you're not insulted."

I smiled indulgently. "Not at all."

After she left, I waited a few minutes for Josh to get off the phone. When I saw him wander back to his desk and sit down, I checked my compact mirror. My hair was shiny and bouncy, no lipstick on my teeth. I looked pretty good actually. Red was a fine color for me. Grandma always said it made my skin look healthy. I ran my hands down my black pencil skirt, straightened my spine, and made my way to his office.

I knocked on the glass door. His eyes bugged when he saw me. He made a beckoning movement with his hand and I went in.

"Hey, Mimi. How's it going?" he said giving me a big grin.

And I thought this was going to be awkward. I forced a smile. "Hey. I wanted to talk to you about something."

He leaned back in his chair, his grin becoming wider. What a tool. "I know. You can't make it to the party, right?"

My eyes widened. "What?"

"You can't make it to out engagement party." He slapped his thigh. "Lillian so called it right," he gloated.

"What?" I repeated like a fool.

"She said no way you were you going out with a guy like Max. He was waaaaay out of your league. She reckoned he was probably a gay friend who'd taken pity on you. She guessed you would be coming into my office sometime this week with some excuse that you couldn't make it."

I swallowed and wished I had closed the blinds. I was wearing my especially sharp and pointy heels, so I could have walked up to him and stabbed him in right in the eyes with my heels. But then, I remembered what one of my teachers told me, a strong woman doesn't exact revenge on her enemies, she moves on and lets Karma do her dirty work for her.

"Don't worry. It's okay. I totally understand. Your pride was hurt. You don't have to come," he finished.

I flashed a fake smile. "I'm sorry to disappoint Lillian, but Max and I are coming. Unless you or Lillian feel it is too awkward. In that case, of course, we won't come. Obviously, we don't want to spoil your special day. We'll probably just stay in and have sex. Max is amazing in bed. Just amazing. It's five times a night at the moment." I gave a laugh. "So good. Like you wouldn't believe."

Josh's eyebrows flew into his hairline, which I realized, was beginning to recede. "No, of course, you must come. It is not awkward at all. Both of us would love to have *both* of you over." Then he smiled. I didn't miss the inflection on the word both. Balls, he didn't believe me.

"Fine. We'll see you there then."

"Yeah. I'll look forward to seeing *both* of you at the party."

"Okay."

"Maybe we can double date sometime."

I wanted to hurl. "What a great idea." I whirled around to leave his room.

"Er…Mimi."

I turned. "Yeah."

"You wanted to ask me something?" His eyes were taunting.

"Yes, of course. That's right." I smiled. "I wanted to ask you if I could take that file over there." I pointed over to a file that I'd brought to him two weeks ago while I was using every excuse in the book to come in here.

"Don't you have a copy on your computer?"

"I accidentally deleted it this morning," I said and walked over to the file. I picked it up, opened it, and pretended to scan through it. "Yup, this is the one." I lifted my head. "Thank you for this." With a smile plastered all over my face, I walked out of his office. I went back to my little cubicle, sat on my chair, and let my head hit the table with a thud.

Shit. I was in so much trouble.

21

MIMI

I stood at my front door until I heard Max in the corridor. I waited until he got into his apartment, then gave him another seven minutes before I went to knock on his door. He opened it and I wanted to swoon. Nobody should look this good at six o'clock in the evening.

I flashed him a bright smile.

He crossed his arms. "Did you bring the five hundred bucks?"

"What?"

"Aren't you here to ask for my help, to go with you to the party?"

"No," I lied. "I told you I'm not going to that…event."

Something flickered in his eyes. He narrowed them. "So what do you want?"

Fine. He wanted to play it that way. Then he deserved everything he got. I looked at him from between my lashes. "Well,

I was thinking…should we be bad? Should we do something sinful together?"

His eyes gleamed with the kind of wickedness that made me want to put it in a safe so I could take it out every now and again to look at.

"You sure you want to go there," he asked. His husky voice had dropped an octave.

"Baby, I'm already there." Wow, I was on a roll.

His eyes widened with surprise. "What were you thinking of?"

I smiled seductively. "Let's eat chocolate cake together."

To my surprise, he didn't react at all. I had led him down the garden path, but he was playing it cool. "Sure," he said softly.

"I'll bake it and bring it over. It'll take me no more than an hour in total. Is that okay with you? Will you still be around?"

"I wouldn't miss it for the world," he said dryly.

"Good. See you soon. I was wearing my pencil skirt and I did have a good ass on me, so I swung it for all I was worth on my walk back to my apartment. I smiled to myself. I must have done a good job because I never heard his door close until I reached mine.

Once I was inside I didn't waste a minute. I made cupcakes using a recipe for a pound cake and just halved all the ingredients. Once I had put them into the oven I started on the icing. As soon as the cakes were ready I took them out transferred them to a plate and stuck them in the freezer for a few minutes.

While they were in the freezer I applied a layer of gloss and fluffed up my hair. When the tops of the cakes were cool, I took them out and iced them. I put them on a decorative plate and carried them to Max's door. I knocked and waited.

"Hello," he said, his eyes sliding to the plate of cupcakes I was holding.

"I come bringing peace offerings," I said with a sweet smile.

"I didn't realize we were at war." His voice was even.

"You know how competitive some New Yorkers can get during a bet. I just wanted to let you know that I'm not like that."

"Bright colors," he commented.

I snickered. "Yeah, artificial food coloring. I know you're a sucker for artificial things."

He crossed his arms over his chest. He had a very, very nice chest. "Is that some kind of dig at the women I bring home?"

I'd seen women go into his flat. Women with big breasts. I smiled brightly. "While we're on the subject of bringing women home, aren't you going to invite me in?"

He stepped aside and I sailed in. I went straight to the kitchen and put the cakes on the highly-polished granite island top. Everything in his kitchen looked brand new. It was clear the man never cooked. I opened the refrigerator and took out a carton of milk. I poured it into two glasses and sat on a stool. He took the one opposite. I pushed the plate towards him.

"It is poisoned?" he asked.

I didn't dignify that question with an answer. Instead, I

reached out for the cake that was closest to me and was about to bring it to my mouth, when he leaned forward, caught my hand, and took that cake himself.

I bit my lip. "Very well," I said and took one of the other cakes.

He waited until I bit into my cake before he sank his perfect teeth into his. "Why this is delicious," he said, sounding surprised.

"I know. It's a secret recipe." I licked the icing and his eyes watched my tongue. When I finished my cake I stood. "Right, I should be going."

He eyed me suspiciously, but said nothing, as he followed me to the door. When I got back home I changed into my jeans and then sat on my toilet seat and waited. Twenty minutes later I heard his toilet flushing. Bingo. I went back to my living room and let the sound of Adele fill the air, but not too loud that I wouldn't be able to hear anyone knocking on my door. Less than ten minutes later I heard not a knock, but a banging.

22

MIMI

I opened the door and found Max standing there. His hair was tousled, his face was pale, and there was a sheen of sweat on his face.

"What's the matter?" I asked.

"Cut the crap," he growled. "What do I do to get rid of it?"

"Do I win the bet?"

He thrust a bunch of fifties towards me.

I don't want money. I want you to take me to the party."

"All right. Hurry up."

I opened the door wider. "Come in and sit down."

I pulled a small dark bottle out of my back jeans pocket and held it out to him.

He gave me the death stare. "How do I take it?"

"Unscrew the cap and drink it."

He looked at the Chinese text on the label. "What the hell is this? Are you sure it's not going to kill me?"

"Why would I kill you? I need you to take me to the party," I said sweetly. "Take it. It's Chinese herbs. It's a bit bitter, but it works almost instantly. My friend brings it for me from Hong Kong. It's brilliant for the runs. Down the whole bottle."

He glared at me as he glugged it all. Then he closed his eyes and lay back on the sofa. Men were such drama queens. It was just a bit of chocolate flavored laxative. I waited five minutes then sat on the sofa opposite him. "Feel better now?"

He opened his eyes. "Slightly," he muttered.

"Good. Want some water."

"You poisoned me," he accused melodramatically

Oh, for God's sakes. "I didn't poison you. I gave you a laxative. So you had to rush to the toilet once. It's not the end of the world. In fact, it could even be a good thing. Clean out all the old crap."

"So, you will cheat to win," he observed, looking like a kicked puppy.

I sighed. "I didn't cheat. You didn't set any rules."

He made a face.

"And I was desperate."

He touched his stomach gingerly.

"If I say sorry, can we call it a truce?" I ventured and he nodded.

"I'm sorry."

He nodded again. I was really starting to like this guy. And that was a bad thing. A very bad thing.

"We really should spend an hour together and discuss this in a mature responsible way. Get our lies straight. You know, where, when, how we met, etc."

"Okay."

"I'll cook for you," I suggested.

He recoiled. He actually recoiled in horror.

I raised both hands. "Okay. Okay. I only offered because you look like you can't cook to save your life."

His eyes widened. "Did you just insult my cooking skills?"

"No. Absolutely not. I'm looking forward to eating your cooking."

"I'm busy for the rest of the week. Tuesday next, seven-thirty okay with you?"

"Great."

He stood and I jumped up. "I'm really sorry," I said as we walked to the door.

He turned and grinned suddenly. "How sorry?"

I took a step back, thrown by the abrupt change in him. I knew I had started it, but I didn't really think it through. "How sorry do you want me to be?" I asked uncertainly.

He stared into my eyes, making my insides melt. "I'll think about it and tell you the next time I see you."

23

MIMI

$\mathcal{M}$y first stop in the entryway was always the mailbox. I pulled a few envelopes out and headed for the elevator. There was a smile on my face when I thought about how well I was doing at work. I could hold my head up high and when I ran into Josh, which was often, I found it easy to act as if I bore no grudge at all. Maybe I didn't. My heart was never in it and I was actually relieved to know the truth.

Tracee was so right. I could do much better than him. I still wasn't sure what I was thinking when I decided to sleep with him. Now when I looked at him, all I saw was a frat boy who'd never grown up. He worked out, but the drinking he did with his buddies kept him slightly soft and a little pudgy. His idea of reading was a Maxim magazine. I had nothing against action movies, but that was all he was willing to watch. Now he was going to be a father. I wasn't sure who I felt worse for, Lillian, the kid, or him.

I hit the elevator button and looked down at my mail. The sight of a handwritten envelope in the middle of bills and junk mail made me forget all about Josh. I opened it as I stepped onto the elevator. There was a ticket inside, along with a note.

I have an extra ticket for tonight's show. Are you free? – Max

I took a closer look at the ticket and gasped. Adele? He had an extra ticket to see Adele? Whoever has an extra ticket to see Adele? And from the looks of it, the seat was only four rows back from the stage. My hands trembled with excitement as I struggled to figure out if it was all a big joke. A little revenge for the laxative trick I played on him.

I hoped he didn't think that what happened at his apartment would happen again. I was so, so drunk when we made out. I wouldn't let myself lose control again. I was soooo off men. I wanted nothing to do with men for years. I had absolutely no intention of hooking up with him. Just imagine having to listen to all his women night after night for the rest of my life. I shivered. No thanks.

I thought of that soul-searing kiss. With him, I could lose my heart, and that would be a very stupid thing to do. Far stupider than going out with Josh.

But…Adele.

I had tried and tried to get tickets, but no go. I couldn't even score seats in the nosebleed section. Nada. And here was Max, handing one over like it was nothing.

If he'd left it in my mailbox, it meant he was probably at home. I screwed up my courage and went up to his door. I had to stay strong. I couldn't fall prey to his cool gray eyes or that magnetic pull that seemed to pulse out of him. Or that sensuous mouth.

When he answered the door, it was with a smile on his face and a cocktail in one hand. "Hey, there." He couldn't have been smoother if he tried. I told myself to keep my eyes off his body. He was wearing sweats, and I could see the outline of his sizeable crown jewels.

"Hey." I held up the ticket. "Are you serious about this?"

He shrugged, a sexy smirk pulling at the corner of his mouth. "Does it look like a real ticket?"

"Yes."

"So, I guess I'm serious."

I looked at it again, then at him. "Who's going? I mean, how many tickets are there?"

"Two."

"You and me?"

"That's about it, yeah."

I couldn't help but tilt my head to the side, eyes narrowed in disbelief. "You're an Adele fan?"

He shrugged. "Who doesn't like Adele?"

"I just can't see you sitting at one of her concerts, is all."

"You will if you come with me tonight." He sipped his amber liquor, unable to keep the smile from his lips. Damn, he was smooth. I had walked right into that one.

"Can I ask a serious question and can you answer honestly?"

He nodded.

"Do I owe you anything for this?"

His eyes narrowed. "Do I come off like the sort of guy who

expects something from a woman when he's just trying to do something nice?"

"No."

"Why do I feel like you're lying?"

He shook his head with disgust and actually started closing his door.

I threw myself against the wood to keep him from shutting it. "All right, all right. Maybe I'm jaded," I admitted, wanting to go slice my throat.

"Jaded. Yes, I know how that feels," he said, but his eyes had lost their twinkle. He was happy when he opened the door and I went and spoiled it.

"I'm just a blundering fool. Don't take it personally, please," I said.

Just to rake me over the coals he took his time while he appeared to think it over. Then he opened the door wider and I almost fell through it. "I guess I can be a nice guy and, you know, put myself in your shoes."

I straightened. "Thanks so much. You're a real sweetheart."

"What can I say?"

I grinned up at him. I was already in a different place. I was thinking of watching Adele sing live. "What time should I be ready?"

24

MAX

I was still grinning like a dope as I closed the door.

I knew Mimi liked Adele because I'd heard an Adele track playing the last time I was in her apartment. Buying the tickets was a safe bet. Even if she had refused, I'd have had no trouble passing them on to someone else. Most people liked Adele.

Except for me.

I didn't hate her. I just didn't have any strong feelings either way. Commercial music was designed to pander to the lowest common dominator: basically, catchy jingles and trash. Give me a good rendition of *Carmina Burana* any day.

I finished my drink and went into the shower. I felt good enough to sing.

If any of my buddies knew what I was doing—basically wooing a girl—they would laugh themselves silly. Couldn't blame them either. If anyone had told me a couple of weeks earlier I'd be sitting through an Adele concert to get into a girl's pants, I would've said someone made chili soup out of his brain.

We were talking about me, after all. Maximus Black. The guy who was allergic to the word relationship. How strange that ever since that day she came to my apartment, I'd found myself doing things that were completely out of character.

I mean, what the fuck? Pretending we were together to help her out. Who was I? Mother Teresa? It was all kinds of crazy, but when I saw that asshole and his crowing girlfriend gang up on her, I couldn't stop myself. No one was bullying her while I was around. She needed somebody to look after her and I was that guy.

If any other woman had pulled that stunt she did with the laxative…she'd be using her tears as lube. But with Mimi, I was putty. I just became more and more intrigued.

Underneath the feisty exterior, she was an innocent sweetheart. She would probably claw and spit at my face if she knew I thought of her that way. She wanted to be a badass, but she was soft at her core. The city hadn't ruined or hardened her. She was the opposite of Bridget and her brigade. They pretended to be helpless on the outside. Inside they were pure steel.

I didn't know why the hell she had that effect on me. What was it about her that made me want to keep trying to get closer? Was it because she seemed to want to stay clear of a relationship with me? Whatever the reason, all I wanted to do was grab her and kiss that plush mouth.

I guess I always had a thing for Mimi, but I resisted it firmly. After I found her shit-faced and slumped on the front steps there was no denying the attraction.

She could pretend all she wanted, but I knew she wanted me too. Hell, it took two people to make out. The way she sucked on my tongue as if it was made from sugar. Fuck, I'd been dangerously close to losing control. I would've kept going if we hadn't been interrupted. It wouldn't have taken anything to lift her up, carry her to the bedroom, and spread her legs open. Even thinking about it now, was giving me a hard-on. I looked down at the raging erection I was sporting. Yeah, there was something about her that got to me.

I'd already been to the gym for a good workout, so I felt pumped and ready for a good night out. It was only a matter of time before I took what was mine. I grinned to myself as I buttoned up the black shirt I'd chosen, then tucked it into my gray slacks.

I knocked on her door at seven sharp. The door opened almost immediately and I had to fucking catch my breath. A simple black dress poured over her generous curves like water. Her long hair hung over one shoulder, curled just a little.

"We match," she whispered shyly.

I found my breath. "No. You're way out of my league. There's no matching you."

She blushed and looked away. I stared in amazement. It was amazing how effortlessly beautiful she was. I wondered if she had any idea. She couldn't possibly not know she was irresistible. Smoking hot body. Big, blue eyes. Full ripe mouth. I could already see my cock disappearing into it.

"Did you call us a cab?" she asked as we walked to the elevator.

"Why would I call us a cab?"

She frowned. "I hope we can find one in time."

"Just because we're not taking a cab doesn't mean I didn't secure transportation. This isn't my first rodeo."

Her lips curved and my cock twitched.

"It's not? Do you have a whole stockpile of concert tickets lying around? Is this part of your normal routine?"

I touched her mouth. Something inside me broke. Hell, she had me on the hook. "Nothing about you is normal."

Her lips parted on a soundless gasp. I took my hand away and she chewed on her bottom lip.

She was like a little girl in a sweet shop inside the limo. I poured champagne into her glass and she insisted on clinking glasses. It was so sweet and old-fashioned. We drank to a great night. She'd never been in a limo, and I was glad to be the first one to give her a ride in one.

I watched her in awe. The curve of her cheek, the color in them, her curving mouth. Her skin glowed and my heart swelled with something unfamiliar.

At the concert she sang every song, cheering, clapping and whooping for three hours. I didn't have to pretend to enjoy it since I'd already confessed Adele was not really my thing. What she didn't know was, I enjoyed the show more than her. I couldn't help but smile through the whole show. It was starring Mimi Young.

The real kicker, the big deal, came after the concert. It was the kiss I left on her upturned cheek after I walked her to her door. I heard her sigh just a little, then I turned and walked away. It killed me to do it, but when I was a kid in short pants, my granddad said, "Always leave 'em wanting more, boy."

"Thanks, Grandad."

25

MIMI

I couldn't stop thinking about Max all day Wednesday and on Thursday. I actually thought I was becoming obsessed with him. I knew I had to stop or I would end up a basket case. Megan called me up on Friday afternoon to see if I wanted to grab dinner with her. I nearly bit her head off in my eagerness to agree. It was a welcome distraction.

The problem was she wanted to talk about Max and the engagement party. She leaned toward me from across the table.

"So, do you know what you're gonna wear?"

"I have no idea. I'll have to dig way back in the closet to find something suitable."

She frowned. "Hang on a sec. You said this is at the St. Regis, right?"

"Yeah. So?" I dug into the bread basket. I was never again making the mistake of drinking on an empty stomach. Bread served in baskets in restaurants was always my greatest weakness. How could it not be? Bleached white flour. It couldn't even pretend to be anything but bad.

"So," she said sternly, "it's probably a pretty swanky event. No offense, but do you have anything that'll hold up?"

I rolled my eyes. "Gee, no offense taken."

"I mean it," she said seriously.

"I know you do. I have a few nice things, but they're more like 'work party' outfits."

"Right. And Josh will already have seen you in both of them." Megan twirled her red curls absentmindedly as she mused.

"Uh, I don't care if he saw me in them. Besides, he's one of the most oblivious people I know so I doubt he'll remember any of my outfits and he'll probably be gazing adoringly at Glamazon to notice."

"Okay, all right. Forget him and what he thinks." She took a sip of her wine, eyeing me up. "What about Max?"

"What about him?" I suddenly became very interested in the menu, even though that was our favorite little Italian restaurant and I could have recited the menu by heart.

"Mm-hmm. I thought so."

"You thought what?" I demanded. "Please, tell me some more about what's going on in my head."

"Why don't you stop kidding yourself, Mimi?" She sat back in her chair and smiled. "You were a total swooning fangirl after the concert."

"Yeah, for Adele."

She laughed. "Adele's not the one who wooed you with champagne and a limo ride. She didn't kiss you on the cheek outside your apartment door, make your toes curl, then walk away and leave you gasping for more."

I blushed, looking around again. "Could you not say such things so loud in public? Please?"

"I'm sorry, but you know it's true. What's wrong with wanting to look nice for him?"

I sighed, playing with my water glass. I couldn't describe how I felt, exactly. "I thought Josh was a trustworthy guy," I finally murmured, still staring into my glass. "I was so wrong. How can I even consider going out with a commitment-phobe like Max? He goes through women like other people go through tissues. One use and he discards them. I don't think I can bear to be discarded just now. My pride is already in tatters."

"Fine, then." She folded her hands, a stern expression settling over her face. "Don't do it for Max or Josh. Do it for you. You deserve to walk into that party feeling gorgeous and fabulous and strong."

I opened my mouth, but nothing came out. I realized she was right. It wasn't about either of them. It was about me showing up there and letting Lillian and Josh know they didn't break me. If she wanted to play games, I'd show her I wouldn't sink to her level. I could be classy and graceful and tasteful.

Megan took my silence for acceptance. "So. When are we going shopping?"

*T*he next time I saw Max was Monday evening when we literally ran into each other. He looked surprised, which told me he hadn't planned it. He approached our front steps from one direction while I came from the other. I wished the ground would open up and swallow me because I was a sweaty mess. He really didn't need to see me in such a state.

Then again, he was sweaty, too.

The difference was he looked sexy. Why was this man so gorgeous? I wondered if there was a single situation in which he wouldn't look like a million bucks. I usually didn't go for guys who had just been out running. Where was the appeal? A sweaty man was a sweaty man. But Max looked good enough to eat, even when the front of his long-sleeved tee was soaked and he was out of breath.

The first thing that came to mind was the thought of him being sweaty and out of breath in bed. Damn hormones, trying to get me in trouble.

"You're a runner?" he asked, taking off his headset.

I shook my head. "Only when I feel like punishing myself." He didn't need to know I was doing all the last-minute working out so that I could tighten up before the party.

He chuckled. "Come on. Exercise isn't punishment."

"So, you *actually* like running?" I asked, cocking one eyebrow.

"Hell, no. I hate it. But all the cool kids are doing it."

I had to laugh because he was right on some level. It seemed like all my friends were runners, even Megan. "Why do you think that is?" I asked as we climbed the stairs together.

"It's the 'in' thing to do. Like organic food, coconut water, and green juice."

"Well, I'm not really an 'in thing' kind of person. I may never run another step unless it's to chase the delivery guy if he forgets part of my order."

He laughed as we got on the elevator. "I think you have the right idea."

I checked him out when he wasn't looking. If running was what gave him that body, I would never discourage him. I couldn't help but admire his thick, toned legs, his firm butt, his broad shoulders, the way I would admire a work of art. And that was all it was, sheer admiration. Just observing and admiring and not fantasizing at all.

I grinned. "I don't like running, but I do like my coconut water. I have a bunch in my fridge. It's one of the best things to drink if you want to hydrate naturally and boy, I sound like a commercial."

He was kind enough to hide his smile. "I'm sold. I'll buy a case."

"Aw, you're so sweet. But seriously, do you want one?"

"Yeah, I'll come over for coconut water." He spoke slowly, quietly. His eyes seemed to bore into me. My skin got all tingly. My skin must be so red.

"I hope you don't think this is, like, a thinly-veiled attempt at seduction," I babbled. *Oh, God, Mimi. Shut your dumb mouth.* Too late. I had already blurted the whole damn thing out.

He blinked, eyes wide like a deer in headlights. "Wow."

"I'm sorry…"

"No, don't be. Wow." He stepped off the elevator, then leaned against the wall. "Not a seduction attempt. And there I was, thinking coconut water was code for something else."

"Could you not, please?" My cheeks burned with the heat of a thousand suns.

"No, really. This is a big moment for me. I never thought of coconut water as an aphrodisiac until this moment."

"I really don't fancy going to prison for killing you."

He grinned. "I'm just disappointed, is all."

"Shut up. I'm going home."

"So, no coconut water?"

I turned around, starting down the hall. "If you really want some…"

He chuckled. "Oh, I want some."

"Coconut water, damn it."

"I know. I really like it. It's my favorite."

I bit my lip hard to keep from laughing as he followed me to my front door. "I have half a mind to tell you to get your own coconut water."

"I could get my own, but I bet yours is better."

I opened my door, holding it open for him against my better judgment. "Careful, or you'll end up drinking it alone."

"Got it." He followed me inside, and I saw him looking around. "This is nice."

I sighed. "Nice is another word for small."

"Big is overrated. It's how you use it."

I thought of myself straddling him and how big and thick he would be under me. "Are we still talking about apartments?"

He smiled slowly. "What do you think?"

Something was happening inside me. "Do you still want that coconut water?"

"Yeah, I do. I came all this way and everything."

I giggled to myself as I pulled two cartons from the fridge, then checked out my reflection in the microwave door before going back to the living room. Not, too bad. Not too bad at all. I found him sitting at the piano.

"Do you play?" I asked, handing him a carton.

"Not a note," he admitted. "I was admiring the piano itself. It's beautiful. Not to sound ancient or anything, but they don't make them like this anymore." He ran his hands over the keys—gently, soundlessly—then closed the lid. "It's really nice."

"Thanks. It was my grandmother's."

"Oh, really? You hauled it all the way up here?"

"Whoever hauled it up here did it when she first moved in," I corrected.

"This was her apartment?"

I nodded, looking around. "This was hers. Sort of my second home when I was growing up. She moved here after my grandfather died. He was still young. Hit by a car on his way out of the office one day."

"Oh, I'm sorry."

"It was really hard for her, even though my mom and aunt were grown up. Their house was too big for her to live in on her own, so she sold it and bought this place."

"And she gave it to you?" He rested his hands on the piano lid. "Along with this?"

I nodded again. "It's sort of all I have to my name, in a way. Actually, more than in a way. It's all I have."

He opened his coconut water and took a long gulp. I had to laugh at the way he grimaced. "I fucking hate coconut water," he admitted, shaking his head.

"No kidding? You hide it so well."

"I keep telling myself I'm wrong about it since so many people like it. I have to be the one who's wrong if it's so popular."

"I feel that way about kale," I admitted.

"Oh, my God! I hate kale!"

"I know! It's disgusting."

"I thought it was just me."

"Me, too."

"So we've both been running and eating kale and drinking coconut water even though we don't like it."

"I actually like coconut water," I reminded him.

"And I secretly like to run."

"Nobody's perfect."

He chuckled, standing. "Thanks for this," he murmured, holding up the carton.

"You don't even like it," I reminded him.

"Yeah, well, it was worth swallowing something disgusting if it meant I got to hang out with you for a minute."

I pressed my lips together. "I've been spending too much time with you," I muttered, shaking my head in disgust.

"Why do you say that?" he asked as he opened the door.

"Because I just thought of a dirty joke to make there."

He paused, thought it over, then smiled before walking out into the hall. "You're learning."

MIMI

*F*or some bizarre, unknown reason, I shaved my legs and bikini line with meticulous care on Tuesday evening. Then, even more inexplicably, I scrubbed my body with a sugar scrub until it glowed. After toweling myself dry, I rubbed my most expensive lavender scented cream into my skin.

Then I chose two of the sexiest bits of cream silk and chocolate lace underwear I owned. The bra had a cute little red love-heart fastener in the front. I spent a long time over my hair too. Carefully putting it into big rollers and gently brushing it out so it fell in bouncy waves around my shoulders.

I slipped into a simple dress because obviously, I didn't want Max to think I had made any effort at all, and cream pumps. A lick of mascara and gloss and I was done. I wanted to look as if I'd just come from work, grabbed the first thing I saw in my wardrobe and put it on, and I think I succeeded. I looked at my phone. Five minutes to seven. I picked up the wine bottle I had bought by the neck and went to knock on Max's door.

It flung open suddenly, and Max filled the threshold. I didn't think I would ever get used to his presence. His hair was a bit wild and his eyes showed definite signs of stress. There was also a strange smell coming from the interior of his home. I raised my eyebrows.

"Everything all right?"

"Sure. Come in."

I held out the wine bottle.

"Thanks," he said and took it from me distractedly. "Take a seat. I won't be long. The food is nearly ready."

Ah, the source of the smell. I smiled and kept my voice happy. "What are we eating?"

"Chicken."

I nodded. "Just chicken?"

He frowned. "No. Of course not. There is a salad too."

"Oh great. I love chicken and salad."

"Can I get you a drink?"

The smell was getting stronger. "Tell you what," I said, cocking my head in the direction of the smell, "why don't we go into the kitchen. You can open the bottle of wine and we can talk while you finish cooking."

He hesitated.

"I love watching people cook," I added with a big grin, and without waiting for him to answer strolled towards the kitchen. The place looked like a tornado had hit it. A far cry from the immaculate state I had always seen it in previously. Casually, I dusted some flour from a stool and took a seat at the island. "Maybe you should check on the state of your dish."

He walked to the oven, donned a pair of black oven gloves, and opened it. A cloud of smoke billowed out as he pulled out a tray of something, well, I had to assume it was food since he was cooking it; although it bore more resemblance to a very large blackened brick than a chicken. I looked at the rectangular charred thing sitting in the middle of the tray with a mixture of surprise. How many days had he been cooking it to burn it that badly?

The smoke alarm went off. He ran and shook a magazine at it, while I got a window open. The alarm stopped after a couple of seconds and both of us gathered in front of the smoking tray.

"What is it?" I asked.

"Buffalo chicken break-away bread," he said gloomily.

There was a recipe book open on the island with a picture of Buffalo chicken break-away bread and I had to admit it looked delicious. "You shouldn't have started with such an ambitious project," I said softly.

"Do you like Chinese?" he muttered.

"Love it."

We called my favorite takeaway joint and I gave Mr. Chan our order.

"You no want a double order of number eight and number sixty-six today?" he asked, surprised.

He was referring to my usual double order of egg rolls, and

his delicious fried bananas and ice cream dessert. Don't get me wrong, I was tempted to add them to the order, but I glanced at Max, and he was looking at me with that look in his eyes. I remembered my nice underwear and said, "Not today, thanks, Mr. Chan."

I hung up and smiled at Max as he walked up to me with a glass of wine.

"Thanks," I said taking it from him. Our fingers brushed and, oh my, my stomach fluttered a little.

He put on some music. Something foreign. I'd never heard it before. A woman was singing. Her voice was high enough to break glass. It must be an acquired taste. We sat next to each other on the soft leather sofa.

"So, tell me, how long have we been seeing each other," he said.

I crinkled my nose. "How about three weeks ago?"

He nodded. "So you were cheating on Josh and me?"

I bit my lip. "Yes."

"Okay. Where did we meet?"

"Let's keep it simple. We met outside the elevator. You said 'Hi' and that was it. One thing led to another and boom."

"Boom," he said softly, his eyes gleaming.

"Boom," I repeated, unable to pull my gaze away, mesmerized by the look on his face. His eyes emitted sparks of promise. I remembered how possessively his mouth had crushed mine and felt the heat between my legs. The room felt like it was spinning. Jesus, how much alcohol had I consumed?

His phone rang. I dragged my eyes away from his and took a big gulp of my wine. He ignored his phone.

"Don't you want to take that call?"

"Nope. What else do I need to know about you?"

"I love shoes."

He nods. "I noticed."

"I run. We both run, obviously. I like my food, but I am constantly on a diet."

He frowns. "Why?"

"You know why."

'No, I don't. I think your figure is perfect. If anything, you could stand to gain a few pounds."

I couldn't help it. I blushed. Oh God! This man sure knew how to say all the right things.

*T*he food arrived. We sat at the table and she looked like she couldn't believe the message inside her fortune cookie.

A closed mouth gathers no feet.

*S*he read it out reluctantly and I sniggered. Then I broke open my cookie and it was her turn to laugh.

The greatest danger could be your stupidity.

*I*t made me smile to see her laugh. It kinda set the tone for the rest of dinner. We were both relaxed and the conversation was easy and spontaneous as we got to know one another. She was snarky and smart and I like that in a woman. There was always that sexual tension between us, but it was simmering below the belt. By the time dinner was over, I was buzzing just from her company. She moved and her dress rode up her thighs. She reached to pull it down, but my hands curled around hers.

"I was enjoying the view, sexy," I drawled, slow and soft.

She licked her lips nervously, but she allowed me to put her hands away.

"Show me," I whispered.

"What?" she whispered back, her blue eyes wide.

"Your sweet little pussy. I've been smelling it all night. It's time I had a taste. Stand up and show it to me."

Her lips parted. I'd watched her suck noodles through those plump lips without reacting, but now liquid fire rushed through my body. God, I seriously wanted this woman. I craved her flesh the way an addict craves his drug. I needed to strip her clothes off and drink from her sweet pussy.

She pushed back her chair and stood. I turned sideways and pulled her so she was standing between my legs. She looked down at me. I reached under her dress. Her skin was warm and silky.

"You're trembling," I murmured.

Her cheeks became pink.

"What are you scared of, baby? You're the sexiest woman I've ever met."

She bit her lip and looked like she didn't believe me.

"You want this, don't you?"

She nodded and I smiled a little. My fingers reached the lacy rim of her little panties. I hooked them into the waistband and slid them down her legs. The scrap of material pooled around her shoes. Using my other hand, I swept all the plates and leftover food away from us.

"Put your ass on the edge of the table and lie back for me, baby," I instructed. She hesitated a second before obeying. I pushed her dress up and spread her legs until I had a perfect view of her freshly shaven pussy. It was pink and so sweet I wanted to cry. She lifted her head, saw the way I was looking at her pussy and became even redder. My cock was so hard it hurt. Her scent filled my nostrils and made my mouth water. I never wanted to eat out a pussy so badly in my life.

"Damn, girl, you're so wet." My voice was hoarse and thick. I leaned forward and swiped my tongue along her pretty slit for a quick lick. Her juices flowed on my tongue. Fuck, I knew she'd taste good, but she tasted like a slice of fucking heaven.

She moaned and lay quietly while I licked her pussy again. And again. Pussy juice coated my tongue and ran down my throat. Her little cunt gaped for me and I dipped my tongue into it. She jerked her hips towards my mouth, desperate and seeking. Her hands came and clawed through my hair.

I sucked her clit into her mouth and I felt her tense up.

"Oh, Max," she groaned and ground her pussy against my mouth.

I carried on sucking until her pussy started to pop, and her cum rolled down my chin.

"I'm coming," she panted. I grabbed her ass cheeks and kept on sucking as her whole body bowed as she came hard in my mouth. I continued to lick her pussy long after she came, just enjoying the taste of her. She was breathing hard when I gave her one last kiss and lifted my head. She got onto her elbow.

"Wow," she whispered, her eyes hooded.

"I want to see your tits." I watched her sit up and take her dress off. Her bra had a fastening in the front and when she flicked it, her breasts sprang loose. That was some rack she had, swollen and heavy with rosy tips. They bounced and begged me to suck them. My stomach clenched, and my erection felt hot and thick in my pants.

Mimi Young, the object of too many fantasies, was naked on my dining table. The number of times I had stroked myself to release thinking of her was too many to count.

I looked at her hungrily. I cupped a breast, felt its delicious weight in my hand. Then I rolled the hard nipple back and forth between my fingers until she groaned, and her body arched. I liked looking at her body completely exposed. I stared at her and experienced a strange sensation. One I'd never had before. Possessiveness blazed inside me.

This was my woman. She was mine and only mine. God help any man who even fucking looked at her.

I leaned forward and bit her nipple. She drew in a startled breath sharply then groaned low—the sound was erotic and primitive. I sucked it hard, and she shivered helplessly. The more I sucked the more she writhed and whimpered like an animal. The sounds she uttered made me feel wild and strangely out of control. She rubbed her open pussy against my clothed shaft. It felt so damn good I nearly came right there. Every nerve, every cell screamed out for me to slam into her. At that moment nothing mattered, except her. Her body. Her mouth. Her pussy. Her cries of pleasure. She was my only reality.

She tore at my shirt, buttons pinging. Her fingers looked pale nestled in my chest hair.

'Oh, yes, Mimi. Oh, yes,' I encouraged.

She began to undo my belt. Her fingers were frantic. All I could think of was the lust I felt for her. I felt as if only she could give me the satisfaction I craved. As if what I would get from her would put every other experience I had had into the shade. My fingers moved in and out of her, maddening her. She unzipped my pants and pulled at my boxers. I couldn't wait to get inside her. Suddenly, my cock was in her hands. She gripped me by the base. A groan rumbled in my chest.

'God! You're so beautiful,' she whispered in awe.

I looked at his cock. It looked like something that had been made from smooth plaster. It was so... mammoth. Every inch was blemish free and flawless. Like a beautiful golden horizontal pillar. I wonder how he will fit inside me. I couldn't wait to impale myself on it. He rolled a condom on it and rubbed the tip of it on my wetness. I closed my eyes with anticipation.

Suddenly my ring tone jerked me out of my frenzy. For a second, it didn't register properly and I froze.

"Leave it," he snarled.

I wanted to leave it, but nobody called me at this time of the night. Megan knew I was with Max so she would never call. Unless it was an emergency. It could be my mother. My mother and I have drifted apart since Grandma died, but I was all she had. My phone continued to ring.

'I can't," I whispered. "It could be an emergency. My mother."

He pulled away from me with an oath of frustration and I

scrambled away. Suddenly I was aware of how naked I was. I grabbed the phone and looked at the screen. For a second I couldn't believe what I was seeing.

Tracee!

What the hell? Why would be she be calling me now? She had never called me anytime after eight. Never. Something must be very wrong with her. I looked at Max. He was staring at me with a disbelieving expression. "I'm sorry I have to take this," I said.

He groaned and lay back down. I took the call.

"Oh, thank God," Tracee cried urgently. She sounded frightened and shaky.

"What's wrong Tracee?" I asked, my blood running cold.

"I'm so sorry to call you, but I, I didn't have anybody else to call."

"It's okay. What is it?"

"It's my brother. I think he's dead."

"What?" I gasped.

"The police just called me. He was in a car accident," she said, her voice trembling uncontrollably. "I have to go and identify the body. They want me to go to the Office of the Chief Medical Examiner. I have the address, but I have no one to go with me," she ends on a sob.

"Oh, Tracee. I'm so sorry. Of course, I'll come with you."

"I'm sorry to ask you, but I really have-"

"Don't worry about it, Tracee. I'm glad to be able to help."

She started sobbing. I couldn't believe this was the Tracee I knew. Cool, calm and collected. I didn't know what to say. "Don't cry, Tracee. Please don't cry. I'll get there as soon as I can."

"Thank you, Mimi." She sniffed. She sounded so grateful I felt sorry for her. "Thank you so much. How long will it take you to get here?"

"I'll call for a cab now."

"Thank you, Mimi. You don't know what this means to me. I hope I didn't wake you up."

"It's okay. No, you didn't."

I asked her to text me her address and hung up. Max walked towards me. He had zipped up his pants and was holding my bra, panties and my dress in his hands.

"Do you want me to come with you?" he asked.

"No. It'll just make her feel uncomfortable." I couldn't look him in the eye. I held my dress against my body like it was a shield.

He leaned forward and kissed me on my forehead. "I'll call you a cab."

When he had turned away I pulled my panties up and slipped my arms into my bra.

I dressed quickly while he was on the phone arranging an Uber ride for me. "I'm sorry," I said.

"No problem," he said, but his eyes glittered.

Max insisted on coming down the elevator with me. He put me into a cab and closed the door.

"Make sure she gets into the building she's going into before you drive away," he told the driver and handed him a twenty.

"Gee, thanks," the guy said.

Max stood on the sidewalk as the car pulled away. I turned to watch him. He looked so broad and tall. I felt confused and dazed.

When I got to Tracee's address she was waiting for me in the lobby of her building. She was wearing jeans and a green sweater. Her hair was disheveled and she looked white and shocked. I could hardly believe she was the same woman I worked for. She was so different.

"Thank you for coming, Mimi. I'm sorry to bring you out here at this time of night." Her voice broke.

"It's okay. I don't mind," I said quickly.

She pressed her forehead with her hand and cried pitifully, "God. How could this have happened? I just saw him last week."

I felt inadequate in the face of her loss and grief. How was I supposed to react to her distress? Should I reach forward and comfort her or just stand there? She had never been a touchy-feely sort of person and she always drew a fine line between us. We were always boss and subordinate. Besides she had a germ aversion.

"Hey, it's okay," I said without attempting to touch her.

She pressed her lips together. "All right, let's go."

30

MIMI

To my surprise, Tracee wasn't taken into a room where a sheet was lifted and she was shown the body. Instead, we were told to wait in a small room. Tracee stood and paced the small room until a woman came in. She was wearing a white blouse and a gray skirt and she carried a clipboard. She shook our hands and introduced herself as Ruth Corwan. She was a Grief Counselor.

"The identification will be through a photo and I'll be with you during the whole process," she explained softly.

"So, I won't have to see my brother's body."

She shook her head gently. "You can take as much time as you need. I will put this clipboard down on the table. The photograph is face down and when you are ready you can turn it over. The photo will show your brother lying down. He has some head trauma, but his face is unmarked. There is also some bruising on his neck."

Tracee nodded slowly and laid her hands on the table with their beautifully manicured pale nails.

"Take as much time as you like," Ruth said softly. "There is no hurry at all. I am here to help you."

"I'm sorry you to have to be here," Tracee said.

Ruth shook her head and smiled kindly. "Don't be sorry. I consider my job an honor and a privilege. Birth and death are natural. Some people are around at the beginning of a person's life and others are there at the end."

Slowly, Tracee lifted one corner of the photo and turned it over. Her brother looked nothing like her. His hair was matted with blood on one side and there was a bruise on his neck, but otherwise, he looked like he was sleeping. For a long time, Tracee stared at the photo. The room was so quiet you could have heard a pin drop. I could hear my own heart.

Then she took a shuddering breath. "Yes, that's Mickey."

The woman reached over and touched Tracee's hand and Tracee jumped and shrank back. An expression of surprised hurt crossed the woman's face and I nearly wanted to tell her about Tracee's germ phobia.

The woman gave Tracee details of where she can go to get counseling and help if she needed and then she stood to leave.

"You can go now if you want," Tracee said to me. Her hands were shaking.

"No, I'll stay with you."

She looked at me gratefully. I stayed with her until she felt well enough to leave. It was nearly three o'clock and the air was chilly outside. I called a cab and dropped her off at her apartment before going back to mine.

I got out of the elevator and walked slowly to my apartment.

I felt strangely drained. Seeing Tracee that way shocked me. Is that the fate that awaited me one day? So alone I have to call one of my staff if I get into a moment of terrible pain?

I kept seeing her white face, her lips trembling.

When I tried to hug her, she stood in the circle of my arms like a piece of wood until suddenly a dam broke inside her and she held me tightly and sobbed like a baby. How lonely her life must be?

I fished out my key and Max's door opened.

"Are you all right?" he asked from across the corridor.

I nodded.

We stood staring at each other for a few seconds. Then he crossed the space between us in great strides and pulled me into his strong arms. I could feel the heat coming from his body, smell his aftershave, and hear the steady beat of his heart. It felt so safe and right. I wanted him so much it hurt, but I knew I couldn't have him.

I felt hot tears start rolling down my face.

I didn't really know why I was crying. I wasn't close to Tracee at all. Maybe it was just the human connection. Her sadness that had temporarily rubbed off on me. He never said a word, until I pulled away from him.

"Do you want to come to my place?" he asked.

I shook my head. I was too confused about everything. Him. My life. My priorities. I knew one thing for sure. I didn't want to be like Tracee fifteen years from now. If I kept hooking up with guys like Josh and Max that was exactly what I was staring at.

"I think it would be a mistake for us to continue seeing each other."

Something flashed in his eyes, but so quickly I couldn't tell what it was, especially the way I was feeling. Then he went still. "Why?"

"I'm too confused about everything. I just broke up with Josh, and I don't even know how I really feel about it. I don't want to go from his bed into yours. I think I need some time to evaluate my life, and where I'm going."

His brows drew down. "Fair enough."

"I'm sorry if I led you on. If you don't want to come to the party with me tomorrow, I'll understand."

"No, I'll take you to it. There's no fucking way I'm giving either of them the satisfaction of having a laugh at your expense."

My heart beat a little faster at the determined expression on his face. "You will?"

He nodded. "Sure I will."

I stared at him. He was so beautiful. I wanted to reach out and touch his unsmiling face. "So we're friends?" Something inside me hurt to ask him that.

He shrugged one shoulder. "Yeah."

"Thank you, Max."

"No problem. See you tomorrow?"

I was too choked up to speak. I just nodded and went into my apartment.

I turned around to close the door and he was just standing there.

"Goodnight, Mimi. Sleep well."

"Goodnight, Max," I whispered. Then I shut the door on him. That night I made up my mind. I would go to the party tomorrow with Max and then that would probably be it for us. The truth was I could never be friends with him. I had complicated things by getting close to him. Now it would kill me to see the parade of women he brought to his apartment. Especially now that I had a taste what he was like as a lover. I wished that he would sell to the developers and move away. I thanked God we had not gone all the way, but the thought made my heart ache.

"*A*re you sure this looks all right?" I turned to the side once again and checked out my almost bare back.

Megan was watching me from the edge of my bed. She smiled at me in the mirror. "I'm gonna need to break out the thesaurus to find compliments I haven't already used."

"I feel like I'm showing too much back."

"What's wrong with showing too much back? You have a sensational back. If it were cut that low in the front, then we'd have to talk."

"If it were cut that low in the front, I'd get arrested." I shook my head, fretting. "Is it a little too much skin for the St. Regis though? I don't want anybody thinking I'm working, and I don't mean as a server."

Megan frowned. "It's sexy obviously, but in a classy, elegant way that would be totally acceptable at the St. Regis."

I faced the mirror again, chewing my lip uncertainly. I was never this insecure.

With an exasperated sigh, she fished through a tote bag full of accessories she'd brought with her. "Here. If it makes you feel better, use this." She wrapped a silver shawl around my shoulders and stood back. It went beautifully with the strappy silver stilettos she lent me after making me promise to care for them like I would my own child. Friendship was friendship, but a good pair of shoes were forever.

I stepped back, taking in the full picture. The dress was navy blue with a halter neck. The front was completely demure and classy, but it was completely backless coming danger-ously close to flirting with the top of my thong. It didn't seem like the dress should stay in place, but it was so beauti-fully tailored it did, even when I sat.

I smoothed down the front of the dress, where it came down to just above my knee. I had to admit; the slim cut hugged my figure and made me feel like squeezing my shoulders forward and blowing sultry kisses like those bombshell movie starlets from the fifties. I wondered what Max would make of this dress. I thought of his burning gray eyes roaming hungrily over my body.

"Where did you go just then?" Megan asked as she plugged in my curling iron.

"Nowhere. I was right here."

"No, you weren't. You looked worried. Are you worried about something? Is it that woman Tracee?"

"No."

"There are lonely, sad people like her in every big city. You're nothing like her."

I nodded. "I know."

"So, what you are worried about?"

"I'm not worried," I denied.

"Bull. Try again."

"I'm…I was…um…thinking. Wondering."

"About Josh?"

"God, no."

"Good, because he's not worth another minute of your life."

"He's not worth my life? Then why am I going to this party again?"

She sat me down on the dining chair she'd pulled into my bedroom and started working on my hair. Her sister was a stylist and had taught her a million tricks, which explained why her natural curls never looked frizzy or unkempt even on windy or humid days.

I draped a towel over my chest and started with my makeup while she separated my hair into sections and pinned it up all over my head.

She waved the curling iron around to make her point. "To show whats-her-face that you're okay. To rise above the mean little shits who seek to drag you down and be gracious in your good fortune."

"Good fortune?"

"She's settling for Josh. You've got Max," she told me.

"I haven't got Max," I reminded.

"She doesn't know that," she said merrily.

"Tonight, you will go out there and enjoy yourself. Show her you're doing just fine." I saw a twinkle in her eye before she continued, "And if you happen to do a little canoodling with a guy about a million times hotter than Josh could be in his wildest dreams, well…"

"There will be no canoodling," I shot back.

"And you wonder why I think of you as an old lady." She rolled her eyes and shook her head with the expression of a disappointed mother.

"You're assuming he'll even want to canoodle with me. I told you, he agreed that we'd be friends."

"Friends, my ass. Honey, when he sees you looking as good as you're going to look when I'm finished with you, you'll be lucky to make it to the party." She winked at me in the mirror.

"I don't think so."

Her sigh echoed throughout the room. "What is it about Max that pushes you away like this? From what you've told me he's funny and charming. And he swooped in to save you when Josh was being an insensitive asshole. I'm sorry, but I don't know why you didn't wake up in his bed this morning."

She doesn't know I very nearly did.

"Well, I guess I'm just going to need to hang around here until he comes and find out for myself."

"Don't you dare," I threatened.

She snorted with laughter. "If you don't think I'm not gonna stick around to get a look at him, you're insane."

I sighed. "Fine, but don't say or do anything that will embarrass me."

"I wonder why he's still unattached."

"Maybe he's got a dead girl in his closet that he cuddles every night."

"Don't be silly. Maybe he's been burned in the past. You know how that feels."

"Or maybe he's obsessed with his mother and no woman will ever measure up."

She laughed. "He's probably too busy for a relationship, or he's waiting for someone as special as you to come along."

"Or the truth. He's a serial womanizer."

"Not everything has to be so serious, Mimi. It's okay for you to have a little fun, you know."

"I can have fun without sex, thanks. Sex with Josh is what got me into this mess. I followed my sex drive and look where it got me." I looked into my best friend's eyes, reflected over my head. "Please, let me heal up a little before I get back out there, okay."

"Of course. You do what feels good to you. I shouldn't push you like I do. I just want you to be happy."

I reach back and touch her hand. "I know you want what's best for me."

"I love you, Mimi."

"I know. I love you too, Megan."

She laughed. "Geez. How the hell did we get here?"

I laughed too. "No idea, but you know what would make me happy right now?"

"What?"

"A whole carton of chocolate ice cream and a pack of cigarettes."

"You haven't smoked since graduation."

"It's never too late to restart a bad habit. I have to do something for my nerves and I can't chew on my nails since I just got them done."

"Just relax and let me work my magic."

And she did, curling and twisting and pinning until my hair was arranged in a curly mass on the back of my head. I couldn't have done something like that in a million years—I'd have burns all over my fingers and a bird's nest to show for it if I tried.

One thing I could do though was makeup. The smoky eye I gave myself looked pretty awesome with scarlet lips.

Megan was right, I thought as I stood up. I looked great. After the damage I did to my credit card with a manicure, pedicure, new dress, and purse, I damn well should. I'd be paying off my night out for a long time, but if I pulled this off with my pride intact, it would be worth it.

There was a little piece of me—maybe more than a little piece—that wanted to make Josh sorry for what he'd done. I wanted him to look at me tonight and regret cheating on me.

"Thanks, Megan," I said touching my hair. "You're like a real-life unicorn. Just too good to be true."

She made an exaggerated bow.

"What time is it?" I asked.

"Three minutes later than when you asked me last time," she muttered, as she cleaned up our mess.

"God, I'm nervous," I said, laying my hand on my stomach.

"There's nothing to be nervous about. You look stunning."

I slid my feet into her five-inch, pencil-thin heels and did a little tour of my bedroom to acclimate myself. "I have butterflies."

"Get over it," she said without turning around.

"Maybe it's nausea."

She whirled. "Don't throw up on the shoes, or I swear to God our friendship is over."

"I'm glad to know where I fall on your list of priorities." I sat down, my knees like jelly. "I can't believe this has me so worked up. I wish I hadn't run into them that day. I wish Max hadn't interfered. I could have just turned them down and that would have been that."

"And what would you be doing tonight instead?" She sat beside me, patting me on the knee.

"I don't know, but I wouldn't be ready to throw up on your shoes. That much I know for sure."

"You're going to a fabulous party, instead," she said firmly. "With a guy who makes you laugh. If nothing else, you will have a great time together. Forget the reason you're even there. Just have fun."

I looked out the window nervously. "What's the weather like outside?"

"And now I'm a meteorologist," she muttered, checking an app on her phone. "It's chilly. Clear. No rain, thank God. I didn't do your hair for nothing."

"What time is it now?" I got up, pacing.

"It's almost eight. He'll be here any minute. Would you please calm down?"

"I don't know what it is," I admitted. "All of Lillian's friends probably know who I am. They know Josh and I were sleeping together. What if they start something with me?"

"You'll call me and I'll get there and kick some ass," she growled. "But I don't think it will come to that. This isn't a revenge story."

"I hope not."

"Besides, you won't be alone. Max knows what's up. He'll protect you. I just have a feeling about him."

As if on cue, the doorbell rang. The sound of the bell must have triggered my bladder since I had to pee all of a sudden, but I didn't dare leave Megan alone with Max—I didn't trust her mouth. She scrambled to her feet to answer while I checked my reflection once more.

"Hi," I heard Max say, surprise in his voice. "I'm here for Mimi."

She didn't reply right away. I turned to see why and instantly understood. He took my breath away, too. Something deep in the pit of my body roared to life, while I pressed my lips together to contain the helpless groan that threatened to slip out of my mouth. I started rethinking my "no sex" rule then and there.

MIMI

J couldn't have described him in all his glory if I tried for a week. There just weren't words in the English language, to describe the aura that seemed to surround him. Gorgeous, sexy, debonair—I could have gone on and on, but it wouldn't have been nearly enough.

All I could do was admire how majestic he looked in his black suit, the collar of his white shirt open at the throat just like it had been that night on the front steps. He wore a black trench coat with a gray scarf that matched his steely eyes. How were other men at the party going to cope with all this masculine perfection?

His eyes shifted from Megan to me, and I wondered if I imagined them widening just a little bit.

"Wow," he breathed.

Every cell in my body tingled at that single sound, that one-syllable word coming from his mouth. I felt the hair on the back of my neck stand to attention. A shiver ran through me as his eyes took me in from head to toe.

"Do I pass muster?" I murmured.

He didn't say a word. He just kept staring.

"So, I'm Megan," my best friend said, still standing at the door. "Nice to meet you."

"Oh!" Max chuckled, then shook her hand. "It's good to meet you. Max Black."

"I know," she said, sounding a little giggly. I told myself that couldn't be her. She was the most together person I knew. Men didn't make her giggle like that. I rarely made her giggle and I was her best damn friend.

"Well, this is great, but I think we should go. We don't want to miss the effigy I'm sure Lillian and her friends are burning in my honor."

I pulled my coat from the rack, and Max was by my side in a moment to help me put it on. Did I imagine his hand lingering on my shoulder? It felt pretty good, imaginary or not.

"I've got your back," Max assured me. "Nobody's burning you in effigy while I'm around."

"I feel so much better now," I joked, but when I looked at him —we were a bit closer in height, thanks to Megan's shoes— he wasn't smiling. He meant it. For once, he was being dead serious.

Megan went into the bedroom to get her things together, leaving me alone with Max for a moment. He looked me up and down again. "Speaking strictly from the friend zone, you look incredible," he said softly.

I felt myself blushing all over and couldn't meet his gaze. The tightening in my chest and core were too much. "You don't look so bad yourself," I said awkwardly. Boy, what an understatement. There should be an award for understatements like that.

"I clean up all right," he shrugged. "But you…"

"You know, you're starting to make me wonder how bad I look the rest of the time," I whispered with a wink.

His eyes gleamed. "I remember what you looked like last night."

I swallowed hard. My decision to stay away from him after tonight was already flying into the danger zone. "Huh, trust you to only remember that."

"Oh, no. I remember all the way back to the night we met."

My heart skipped a beat when I heard the intimate tone of his voice. Was I kidding myself? Because he was sounding like he was really into me. Unless it was just his technique. I stared into his eyes. I wanted to make a joke. Say something funny, break the tension, but I was completely tongue-tied.

"All right, kids. Have fun," Megan said, putting on her coat as she walked through the living room. She was not looking at either of us. I could already imagine what was going on in her head. I might as well clear a huge chunk of tomorrow to make time for the marathon phone call we'd have.

"We're out of here too. We'll take the elevator together," Max suggested. I almost wished he'd let her go since I suddenly wanted to be alone with him. I wanted him to look at me the way he had when he first saw me, as I tingled and shivered and felt warm all over. I decided my credit card could handle the damage if it meant him looking at me that way.

The three of us left the apartment and walked down the hall.

Max chatted with Megan. Once she got over that first surge of blood to her brain at the sight of him—I knew how that went since I felt the same way when I saw him in that suit and coat—she more than held her own. As always, she was witty and funny and interesting. I wished I could be like her.

Still, even though he talked with her, his hand was on my elbow as we left the building.

"Have a great night," Megan called out. I threw a glance her way as I climbed into the limo—yes, another limo—and she gave me two thumbs up. Then, when Max wasn't looking, she fanned herself and while rounding her eyes and panting. I rolled my eyes and the limo pulled away from the curb.

"She seems nice," Max said with a smile.

"She's the best." But I wasn't smiling. It hit me harder than ever that we were heading into the belly of the beast. I hoped it wouldn't be as bad as I kept imagining it.

"You'll be fine," he said, reading my mind. His hand touched mine, tentatively at first. When I didn't pull away, his fingers closed over mine and squeezed, gently. A lightning bolt traveled up my arm and all through my body. "We'll have a good time."

"I hope you're right," I breathed, my heart racing. I told myself it was only nerves and not his touch.

MIMI

*M*ax held his hand out to help me out of the limo. He didn't let go when we stood nearly eye-to-eye.

"I didn't realize how tall you are," he said softly.

"It's the shoes, of course."

He leaned forward just the smallest bit, and for one breathless moment, I thought he was going to kiss me right there on the sidewalk, but of course, he didn't and I couldn't help the jab of disappointed that filled my heart.

We turned to face the hotel. The red-carpeted steps leading to gold-trimmed doors reeked of glamor and luxury. That was exactly why I was surprised that Josh was holding his party here.

Doormen nodded at Max and he nodded back. "Have you ever been here before?" Max asked as we walked up the steps.

"Never. This is a little high-rent for my taste."

"You live in a high-rent area."

"My grandmother did," I reminded him, as the bellmen inside started spinning the heavy revolving doors.

"Of course," he said smoothly as he joined me inside.

"Thank you, Mr. Black," the bellman said, as Max slipped him a tip.

"I guess that means you've been here before?" I said.

"A few times," Max replied, sounding like it was no big deal. Right. No big deal, indeed. I almost fell over when I looked around and saw what we'd just walked into.

"Jeez, Louise," I whispered, looking around. It was pure indulgence with marble everywhere, the lofty ceiling had a mural of blue skies and cherubs. Even the post box was gilded in gold with a stunning carving of an eagle perched on the top of it.

Max snorted. "Do people still say that?"

"I just did." I ignored his attitude and feasted my eyes on the marble floors, the high ceilings, gold trimmed everything. The chandeliers sparkled, the floors shone. It was like stepping into a palace. I realized I'd stopped dead in my tracks and felt embarrassed. "I'm like a country bumpkin," I muttered.

He smiled indulgently. "It's sorta cute."

"I'm not going for cute tonight," I reminded him.

He took my arm. "No, you've gone for ravishing and nailed it."

"I still feel like I'm in way over my head all of a sudden," I admitted.

"Why? Because of all this?" He waved a dismissive hand as we walked slowly in the direction of the elevator. "Don't let this get to you. It's just a place. Anybody with enough money can rent a ballroom for the night. So what?"

"So, I'm not used to things like this. Especially not when I'm going to my ex's engagement party."

"Stop thinking of him as your ex," Max advised, and he wasn't joking for once. "He's one of your managers. You work with him. That's it."

"Okay, you're right. I have to change my mindset."

"Besides, I'm the one you should be focusing in on tonight," he reminded me.

"Huh?" We stepped into the elevator. I was glad we were the only two in there.

"I'm your boyfriend, remember?" He flashed one of his patented sexy smirks and my stomach did a slow flip-flop.

"Oh, right. Damn it, I forgot all about that."

He grinned. "You're breaking my heart, baby."

I grinned back. "I can't help it if you're a forgettable person."

He snapped his fingers, looking rueful. "And I thought my grandpa keeps forgetting my name because he's senile. Now I know better."

I shook my head. It was impossible to stay serious when I was with him, but I needed to be serious just then. "What should we do now? I mean, how should we act?"

"Like we're in love," he murmured, and I gasped softly when I felt his hands on my waist. He pulled me in just a little, just until our bodies touched. His eyes searched my face before locking with mine. I couldn't breathe. All the air left the wood-paneled elevator car. The doors would open and they'd find me passed out on the floor. Or dead, because my heart stopped. Either way, there would be one less person at the party. Josh could use the money I saved him to buy a wreath for my funeral.

"Right. We're in love. We're in love." My voice shook a little when I spoke.

"Careful," he whispered with a sly smile. "Say that enough times, and it could come true."

My heart skipped a beat. "I could never be in love with a man who enjoys running. I'm sorry."

When the doors opened, we were both laughing. That was a good start, I decided. We looked like a happy couple.

We stepped into the ballroom together, and I was successful in holding back my utter amazement. The vaulted ceiling was dappled with big, fluffy clouds and dotted with gorgeous, golden chandeliers that cast their glamorous light over the room.

"For an engagement party, they really went all out. I would think this was a reception if I didn't know any better." I looked around, taking it all in. The flowers, candlelight on every high-top table around the perimeter of the room. The band playing quietly in one corner.

"Hard to imagine how the wedding could top this," Max agreed. "You can tell me all about it."

"Oh, if you think I'm going to their wedding, you're out of your damn mind."

He laughed as he helped me out of my coat. "Come on. I'll go if you will. It might be a lot of fun. Plenty of people watching."

"I can do that by sitting on my front steps without having to wear a fake smile for hours on end. Thanks, but no thanks." I'd decided to go without Megan's wrap and felt the air on my back once my coat was gone. Then I noticed the degree of near-nudity some of the other women had gone for. It was like they were having a contest to see who could look more naked. I saw more side-boob in that ballroom than I usually did watching the Academy Award red carpet pre-show.

35

MIMI

J scanned the room while Max checked our coats, noticing the air kisses and squeals of joy as friends who'd probably just seen each other earlier in the day greeted one another like they'd been on opposite sides of the world for years. I was gladder than ever that Megan kept it real.

The sensation of Max's hand on my bare back snapped me to attention. "Shall we?"

"I don't know. You sure we can pull this off?"

"Just follow my lead."

"Okay," I whispered.

He leaned in and murmured in my ear. "I think you're the most beautiful woman here. No contest. And I'll bet my bottom dollar you're going to go in there and show them how much happier you are without that ridiculous ass in your life."

I couldn't help myself. He was so close and saying all the

right things and damn, his hand was touching my bare skin and I wanted him to move lower and I was pretty sure his cologne was hypnotizing me. Before I knew it, I turned my head and kissed him—chastely, gently, like a girlfriend would kiss her boyfriend before heading into a group of people. His palm pressed just a little harder into my back as I did.

"Thank you," I whispered, my skin still tingling where he'd touched me.

"See, if you keep that up..." he murmured, his eyes half-closed, a smile playing on his lips when we parted.

"Keep what up?" I said innocently.

"My cock. You're keeping my cock up with that behavior."

"That is very uncivilized of you, Mr. Black," I mock scolded.

"Yup, that's it. I'm just your regular dick swinging caveman."

"Luckily for you, I've got a thing for cavemen." Was I really doing it? Was I flirting with him? And I was doing a pretty good job, too. That was the craziest part. He made me feel witty and beautiful just by treating me as though I was. I realized as we started making our way around the room with my hand in his, that I felt confident enough to take on anything the night could throw at me.

Good thing, too, since the first person to greet us was none other than Josh. Max squeezed my hand before shaking his. "Good to see you again," he said with a wide smile.

"Yeah, you too."

Josh looked at me and his eyes widened to holy cow proportions. I could tell he was no longer sure how to act. He had been so sure Lillian was right that Max was gay and pretending to help me to save face, but now the ground was slipping underneath him.

He could pretend to be the ultra-confident wunderkind of the financial planning world, but I knew him better than that. He worried all the time that he was a phony and that eventually he'd be found out by people smarter and more talented than him. Right then, I looked at him as he really was. Standing beside Max, he looked downright ugly. Outside and inside. I was amazed at what I'd ever seen in him.

"This is a great party," I said smoothly, glancing around the room. "You really went all out, didn't you?"

"Oh, this had nothing to do with me," he said, looking sheepish. "This is all Lillian."

"I hope that's not a shadow of things to come," Max joked. Only I knew he wasn't joking. I squeezed his hand, hard.

"What do you mean?" Josh asked, his smile slipping. He knew it wasn't a compliment, but he didn't quite get the jab. He wasn't always the sharpest knife in social situations.

I scrambled to beat Max before he delivered the fatal blow. "Oh, you know how it is. If we women left things like this to our men, they'd never get it done right." I beamed at Max, while my eyes sent warning signals. As much as I loved seeing Josh squirm—and I really, truly loved it more than dark chocolate and wine combined—the last thing I wanted to do was make office life even more uncomfortable.

"She's right," Max grinned affably. "I could never pull off planning something like this. Just give me the bill, huh?"

"Oh, my future in-laws paid for everything." Josh shrugged, that sheepish look still on his face.

I winced at Josh for falling so easily into Max's trap and was just about to open my mouth to change the subject when Lillian found us. She gave me a completely fake smile before turning to Josh.

"I was looking for you," she told him in a tone that reminded me of a mother talking to her toddler.

"Sorry. I was just greeting our guests."

She looked at him meaningfully. "My parents want you to meet their oldest friends."

She turned to us, her eyes lingering on Max longer than they should have before she pulled Josh away with her. For a bride to be she looked and sounded very hostile.

We watched as she led him to a humorless group of four. I almost felt sorry for Josh. Without even trying, Max had exposed him for what he was: a weak little boy with no say in his own life. And he would never have a say as long as he was with Lillian. I noticed her brushing her hand over his collar like she was adjusting it before sliding her arm through his.

Max noticed, too. "Poor sucker," he muttered.

"*Y*ou think he's a sucker?"

"Don't you?"

"A bit, but you might want to plug up that leak," I whispered, looking around to be sure we weren't overheard. It didn't look as though anybody was paying us attention. They were too busy having a fabulous time to listen to our conversation.

He raised an eyebrow. "What leak?"

"Contempt. It's leaking out of your voice."

He chuckled. "Okay, I'll play nice. He is an idiot though."

We both accepted champagne from a passing waiter with a silver tray balanced on one hand. "Why do you think that? Just out of curiosity. How would you sum him up?"

His steely eyes narrowed in suspicion. "Why do I feel like you're setting me up? Or testing me?"

"Oh, it's totally a test." I wanted to know more about him, what he thought about things, how he saw the world.

He rolled his eyes but answered anyway. "I'd bet anything that he started dating her because it made Mommy and Daddy happy. She's beautiful, don't get me wrong, but he would have asked her to marry him if she looked like the back end of a bus."

That hurt. "She's beautiful, huh?"

"Are you jealous?"

"No," I said immediately. "Why would I be?"

He grinned. "What else did I say after that line?"

I blinked. "You said something after that?"

His eyes softened and he touched my nose with his pointer finger. "Yes, I did. Anyway, she's not who he really wants, even though she might be who he needs—somebody to push him around and tell him what to do and how to do it since he can't make a decision for himself."

"Oh! Who does he really want?" I just couldn't help it. My hurt pride needed to hear it.

"You." His voice had dropped an octave. I told myself the throbbing between my legs was just the champagne kicking in.

He put an arm around my waist. I let him since it was what he was supposed to do as my fake boyfriend for the night. "But he can't have you anymore because I've got you now."

"Now you're going too far," I murmured, blushing furiously.

"No, I'm not. We have an audience," he whispered.

My breath caught. "We do?"

"Absolutely." He grinned wolfishly. "Now would be a good

time to act as if you're crazy about me." As if it was totally natural for him to have his arms around my waist and pulled me in closer. I told myself to go with it—we were playing a role together, after all—but it was so hard to not act like a fluttery, nervous twit when I could feel his hard body pressed into me. Was Josh watching? I hoped like hell that he was. Lillian watching would be a bonus.

I stared into his beautiful eyes and licked my lips.

"If you keep doing that I'm going to have to take you into the toilets and fuck you until you scream. Then there would be no more doubt that I am your boyfriend."

"Oh, you're so romantic," I murmured. Some part of me wanted so much to think we were not pretending. This was all real. We were an item, flirting and having fun.

He kissed my forehead, his mouth lingering there for the briefest of moments. "You taste of makeup." His breath was cool and smelt of champagne.

I pretended to scowl. "Duh. Did you think I got this flawless look on my own?"

"I liked you just fine without the lick of paint."

I fluttered my eyelashes. "Oh, Mr. Black, you say the nicest things."

"And you, Miss Young, are looking for trouble."

I bit my lip. I loved the idea of being in trouble with him. "You were in the middle of summing Josh up when we were interrupted," I croaked.

His eyes lost their gleam. "There's not much more to say about him. He didn't have the balls to break it off with his meal ticket when he had you. Now that she's turned up pregnant, he's stuck with her for the foreseeable future, even if the marriage is hell on earth, which it probably will be."

"Wow. That's really sad." I placed a hand on his chest because what the hell. I was his fake girlfriend. And oh, I liked touching warm steel. I felt the beating of his heart under my fingertips. I could get used to the whole fake relationship racket if it meant getting to touch him like that.

He frowned. "You're not feeling sorry for him, are you?"

"Right now? No. He still cheated and used me. He didn't have to lie like that, but I can't get too angry because I can't help feeling as if I dodged a bullet with this one."

And I wouldn't be here with you, with your arm around me and your face so close to mine and, boy, are you a good actor because I would swear we were really dating if I happened to see us from across the room. Hell, do you know how good you smell, and how much I want to take your shirt off right now?

He smiled softly. "I guess you did. I'm glad I was there when it happened, even if you were a completely sloppy drunk."

I gasped and was just about to sling a retort when a male voice broke in. "I thought that was you!"

*W*e both turned to find Alexander Fields, CEO, and owner of my firm, standing in front of us. I was flabbergasted. I didn't even know the man knew me. I was sure he couldn't pick me out of a lineup with a gun pointed at his temple.

I opened my mouth to say something, anything, when Max said, "Alex. How nice to see you here. I didn't expect to."

"I could say the same. This is not exactly your scene." His voice was warm and friendly. I noticed the enthusiasm with which he shook Max's hand. I wondered how he knew my boss. The man was a mystery to me. Suddenly, I felt like the outsider. As much as Max pretended that it was us against them. This was his world too. I found myself looking at Max in a different light.

"So what are you doing here?" Alexander Fields asked.

Max's arm snaked around my waist again. "You haven't met my girlfriend, Mimi, have you? She…er…works with Josh."

My boss's eyebrows jumped before his dark eyes fell on me. "Oh, of course. Mimi. It's so good to see you here tonight. You look lovely." I could tell the old guy had absolutely no idea who I was. Max could have told him my name was Britney Spears and he probably would have gone along with it.

I smiled politely. "Thank you, Sir."

Worlds were colliding before my very eyes and I had no idea what to do about it. Nobody in their right mind wanted to make small talk with their boss at a party, especially if their boss had no idea who they were. Not that I held it against him—we were a big firm with plenty of departments, and he was a busy man. However, I couldn't help feeling a little disheartened by the fact that my boss had now been pulled into this charade.

Mr. Fields slapped Max on his back. "Maximus, my boy, this is a providential meeting," His eyes had lit up behind his wire-rimmed glasses. "We're spending this weekend in the Hamptons. Why don't you join us? It would be wonderful to have you out there." He looked at me. "Both of you, of course. Millicent and I would be delighted."

My stomach got that empty feeling it did when I was on a roller coaster. I looked at Max. He looked at me and raised his eyebrow. I blinked to indicate that he should refuse.

At that moment, Josh and Lillian wandered over, hand in hand. Of course—Josh never missed the opportunity to brown nose with his boss.

Alexander motioned for them to come closer. "You, too, Josh. If you're not doing anything this weekend please, come out to the Hamptons and spend it with us. It'll be great."

"We would love to, Alex," Lillian cooed, managing to give me a dirty look while snuggling up to Josh. Josh, much in his fashion, looked like he'd missed the boat again.

"Well, Maximus? What say you?" my boss asked turning his attention back to Max.

Both Josh and Lillian looked at Max, and Max looked at me with a questioning look in his eyes. He was waiting for me to refuse. Dozens of excuses flew through my head. I was getting a root canal. I was repainting my apartment. I was scheduled to contract a contagious illness before then. Anything to get out of spending an entire weekend with my boss and the couple of the evening. For a fraction of a second, I even considered exposing myself to a contagious disease to get out of it. Was bird flu still a thing?

But the simple fact was, I couldn't say no to my boss. It would be ungracious not to mention career suicide. Max had to say no for us. He must know we couldn't go. I raised my eyebrows surreptitiously at him and willed him to find a gentle way of letting my boss down.

"I'm game if you are, sweetie," he said softly.

I reminded myself to push him in front of a bus, or at least hurt him when we were alone again. Then my lips stretched and the words came through clenched teeth. "Of course, I'd love to."

I managed to wait until we were in the limo to lose my cool. "Do you have a paper bag for me to hyperventilate into? Or maybe a loaded gun that I can empty into the side of my head?"

Max stared at me, oblivious. "You're that upset? Why?"

"Are you crazy? You couldn't have told him that it was short notice and we have something else to do this weekend?"

Max settled into the seat. "So why didn't you say it?" he challenged.

"I couldn't turn him down. How could I? He's my boss," I wailed.

"Okay, okay, He put me on the spot! And you staring at me with those big eyes didn't exactly help either."

"What? Are you trying to blame me?" I spluttered.

"It's hard to think when you have a boner," he said cockily.

"It's all a joke to you, isn't it?" I accused furiously. My hand itched to slap that smug expression off his handsome face.

"Oh, come on, Mimi. Lighten up. It won't be so bad."

"Won't be so bad? How do you figure that? A weekend with my boss who doesn't even know who I am. What could we add to make that more uncomfortable and awkward? Oh, right! My ex and his new fiancée who hates me," I groaned, eyes closed.

"You should view this as a great opportunity to get to know your boss. Other people would kill for a chance like this."

I opened my eyes. "You're kidding, right?"

"No," he says seriously.

I shake my head. He didn't understand. I didn't want to get to know my boss in this way. And I definitely didn't want to spend any time at all with Josh or Lillian. I chewed my thumb and tried to think. "Maybe you can go alone. The invitation was obviously for you. Mr. Fields didn't even know who I was until you introduced me." I looked over at him from the corner of my eye. "Very masterfully accomplished, by the way."

"Yeah, well, I can be smooth when I try."

"You could have tried harder back there, Mr. Smooth."

"I don't see why you couldn't have said you were tied up," he argued.

"I didn't want to be rude!"

"Neither did I! Going on my own is going to be useless since Josh will be there. Unless you want him to think we broke up."

I exhaled. "I guess there's no way around this, huh?"

"If I didn't know better, I'd think you didn't want to spend the weekend with me."

"Everything isn't about you, you narcissist."

"I'd resent that if I didn't already know I was one."

"Shut up. You can't charm your way out of me being annoyed with you." I folded my arms, swinging one of my legs back and forth.

"Wow. It's like we're actually a couple. We leave a party and you're pissed at me for something I said inside." He looked at me with one eyebrow cocked. "I mean, if I'm going to go through this kind of grief, I should at least get something out of it."

"Just adorable." I groaned.

"Is that a yes?" he asked hopefully.

I glared at him. "Don't change the subject. This is serious."

He sighed.

"It's one thing to pretend to be together for a few hours at a party, but a whole weekend?" Then another, more startling thought gripped me. My eyes widened. "Oh! My! God! We'll have to share a room. One bedroom. Just the two of us in one bedroom. With one bed."

A wicked gleam shone in his eyes. "I don't think you should panic about that. Most girls enjoy their time in my bed."

I rolled my eyes and huffed. "Really full of yourself, aren't you?"

"You should know since by your own admission you've been listening from the other side of my bedroom wall."

"God, you can be such an ass."

His eyes crinkled at the corners. "I have been called donkey once or twice."

I stared at him in disbelief. "How can you joke about the size of your penis when we are in this mess? How are we going to pull this off? We'll have to act like we're…crazy about each other for a whole weekend."

He flicked his wrist. "It's no problem for me."

"Really?"

"Sure."

"All right. We'll just have to learn more about each other. Like in that movie Green Card."

He looked at me without comprehension. "It was a great movie. I cried. This couple had to pretend to be in love and get married so that the guy could get a green card." I sighed thinking of the movie. "We have to act like we're in love too."

He shrugged. "I think they'll be satisfied with us being in lust."

"What if they get us separately and grill us and our answers don't match?"

"You have a very strange idea of what people do on weekends in the Hamptons."

"I just want us to be convincing, is all. I would hate for them to find out we're lying. That would be too humiliating for words."

He nodded gravely. "Understandable."

"Right. Let's get to know each other better." I turned abruptly to face him. "How do you know Alexander Fields?"

"He's not really my friend." He wouldn't meet my eyes, I noticed.

I narrowed my eyes. "It sure seemed like he knew you very well. Unless strangers regularly invite you to their weekend retreats."

"I have a very trustworthy face. It's a real problem. I can't get a weekend to myself."

I stared at him. "I mean it. Why did he invite you if you don't know each other?"

He sighed, rubbing his hand over the side of his face. "He's friends with my parents, okay? He handles my father's financial planning, that sort of thing. They've known each other for years."

"Oh, I see. I should have known."

"Known what?"

39

MIMI

"You're old money, aren't you?" I said almost accusingly. For Mr. Fields himself to handle his father's financial affairs means Max's family must be in the super wealthy category.

He frowned. "So?"

I looked out of the window. "So nothing."

"So you make it sound like that's a bad thing."

"It's not. I'm just saying, I should have known. The apartment, the limo, all that."

He shrugged it off. "Anyway, that's how Alex knows me. I had to call him Uncle Alex when I was a kid."

I tried to keep my face stoic, but despite my best efforts, it was cracking up. "So he could tell me all sorts of embarrassing stories about you?"

"You already know my most embarrassing story. Or were you too hammered to remember?" he teased.

"Oh, I could never forget something like that even if you pickled my brain in industrial strength alcohol."

"Thanks," he said dryly.

We pulled up in front of our building, and I waited while Max walked around the car to let me out. There we were again, face to face. It was impossible to stay annoyed with him when he smiled the way he did or looked like he did, or oh, jeez, he smelled so damn good. It wasn't fair.

After a breathless moment, when I didn't know whether to swoon or kiss him, he murmured, "You know what?"

"No. What?"

"I think we should go out for dinner tomorrow night at seven." He walked up the steps, leaving me standing alone. I followed him, clomping up behind him like a horse.

"You do? Why?"

He smiled as he held the door for me. "Because we need to get to know one another and I usually get hungry around seven o'clock."

"But I get hungry at six."

"See. That's one more thing we know about each other."

I grinned. "Maybe I could eat a later lunch than usual."

"That's so generous. Maybe I'll pay for dinner, then." We waited for the elevator, and I wished it would never come. I could have stood there in that moment forever. My entire body pulsed in time with my heart.

"Oh, you know you're paying for dinner, buddy. If you can afford a limo, you can afford my dinner."

He looked at me funny. "I should warn you of one thing."

"What?" I asked cautiously.

"Guys expect a little something after they pay for dinner. That's just how the world works." He winked.

I crossed my arms over my chest. "I said friends, not friends with benefits. So you can forget any ideas of finishing the night off with a bang."

"It was worth a try," he mumbled glumly.

I ignored the downtrodden face and kept my voice bright. "I know let's go somewhere I don't have to dress up."

"I'll take you to the worst dive bar for the greasiest food imaginable. How's that sound?"

"Now you're talking."

We laughed as we walked down the hall. I liked how he walked me to my door. I was pretty sure the night couldn't have gone better. We made the perfect couple, even if we were a complete fake. I would never forget the looks on the faces of the other girls at the party. Envy. Straight-up 'I want to claw your eyes out' envy. They all wanted him.

"It's sort of creepy up here sometimes, isn't it?" I said.

"What do you mean?" he asked as we reached my door.

"Just the two of us, on opposites sides of the floor the way we are. The silence is spooky, almost."

I fished in my purse for my keys. "Do you wanna come in for a minute? This conversation is fascinating, but there are Megan's shoes and if I don't get out of these shoes in ten seconds…"

He nodded and followed me inside. I took off the shoes before I even removed my coat, sighing in satisfaction once my bare soles hit the floor. "I swear to God, how Megan manages those medieval torture devices is beyond me."

"You were wearing pretty dangerous shoes the night we met," he reminded me.

"They weren't as uncomfortable as them." I glared at the shoes, lying on the floor. I took off my coat and invited him to take his off, too. He sat on the couch and watched as I removed my earrings and bracelet. I liked the rapport between us. It felt natural.

"Like I was saying, it's sorta spooky sometimes. So quiet."

He grinned. "Until I bring a girl home, that is."

That hurt somehow. I pretended to smile carelessly. "I haven't heard any activity for the past few days. Have you moved your bed?"

"Nope."

My heart damn near soared out of my chest and burst into a million shining pieces of pure joy. I turned my face away so he won't see how happy I was.

40

MIMI

"*A*ctually," he said, "I kind of like the solitude. Maybe I'm too used to it, now. I don't know that I could go back to living in the middle of a bunch of people ever again."

"Are you sure you're not just telling yourself that?"

He shook his head and jerked his chin towards the window. "I get enough noise out there. Besides, there are all those voices in my head, too."

I laughed and sat on the piano bench, facing him. "That explains so much."

"Seriously, though. There are more than enough people out there. This is where I get a little peace and quiet. I can hear myself think."

I chewed on the side of my mouth and mulled over what he said. "I guess you're right. I never thought about it that way. I'm so used to the relentless noise, the police sirens, the traffic, the sound of people's voices, that pure silence actually feels odd."

He stared at me. "I'll have to take you to my ranch in Iowa, where you hear nothing, not one thing, at night. It's the most wonderful thing."

The hairs on my hands stood because I wanted that dream of a silent night on his ranch in Iowa so much. Then my mouth opened and I began to babble out stupid, goofy things I would never say otherwise.

"I guess you're right. There are benefits to living on an otherwise empty floor. It's just you, and a bunch of empty apartments so you can play your music as loudly as you want, or have a massive party without the people next door pissing and moaning about it."

He looked around. "This apartment is too small for a massive party."

"It's not that small," I said, defensive. "We can't all have big, roomy places like you, Mr. My Parents Need a Financial Advisor."

"Ooh, touchy."

"No. I actually don't mind being poor."

"You're not poor. You have this apartment."

I shrugged. "It's worth nothing to me while I live in it."

He nodded thoughtfully. "They must have made you a crazy offer by now. Why didn't you sell? You could buy a much better apartment somewhere else."

"I promised my grandmother I wouldn't sell. She was strangely insistent about it. When she was dying she actually grabbed my wrist and told me that if I sold this apartment I would live to regret it."

He looked at me curiously. "That's intense. Why?"

"I don't know. I asked her once and she just said, 'It's your fortune. It's my gift to you.' It's not even like it's been in my family forever or anything. She bought this house with my grandfather's life insurance and the savings he left her. She left only enough to make ends meet forever. She should have left this apartment to my Mom, but she didn't want to."

I leaned against the piano, my chin in my hand.

"Did she ever teach you to play that thing?" he asked, motioning to the piano.

"She tried very hard but failed," I grinned. "I'm tone deaf. I guess I learned a few songs, but nobody would ever mistake me for a concert pianist."

"Do you remember anything?" He stood, joining me there.

"Maybe."

"Play me something. Please."

"No!" I waved him off.

"Come on. Just one song."

"I'm out of practice."

"This isn't a talent show. I just want to hear you play." He sat beside me on the bench, and I wondered what it would be like to really go out with a man like him.

"All right, but..." I turned around, trying to ignore the little thrill I felt at his nearness. "Do not, under penalty of death, laugh at me when I screw up."

"I won't." He looked amused.

"Swear it."

"Oh, for fuck's sake. You want a blood oath?"

I kept my expression straight.

He chuckled. "Okay. I swear."

I cracked my knuckles, then wiggled my fingers. "Nothing like feeling put on the spot," I muttered, before touching the keys. I thought about *Chopsticks*, but for some strange reason decided to go with my grandmother's favorite. She was a massive Sinatra fan. I haven't played this since she died.

"Fly me to the moon," I half-sang, half-whispered as I played slowly. Very slowly. My voice wasn't much, but I could carry a tune. *"And let me play among the stars...Let me see what spring is like on Jupiter and Mars..."* I then hummed the rest as I played, concentrating on the keys instead of the lyrics as I fumbled my way through. I felt his eyes on me and struggled to focus regardless, even though color rushed to my cheeks, and I couldn't wipe the nervous smile from my face.

I stopped after the first verse. "It's just the same thing over and over," I mumbled, looking down at the keys.

"I know. My mom's a huge Sinatra fan."

"Really? And I just slaughtered that song."

"You didn't. It was really nice."

"Nice is another word for not great," I giggled, remembering his first visit to the apartment.

"Not this time."

I lifted my eyes from the piano keys and dared a look at him. His smile was warm and genuine. If he only knew how close I was to throwing myself at him.

"I'd better go," he said, standing like the bench had suddenly caught fire.

"Oh, do I smell?" I forced a tiny laugh, trying to cover up my crazy thoughts.

"Not any more than usual," he quipped with a wink. "I just remembered I have something to do early in the morning."

"What?"

He chuckled. "I have a meeting, actually."

"You're just going to look at pictures of baby goats on the Internet, aren't you?"

He gave me the side-eye. "You're strange."

"You don't like baby goats?"

"They are almost as cute as you."

God, I so wanted this man. But no. I told Megan I wouldn't, couldn't. It would ruin everything if we slept together. I liked him as a person, which would have to be enough.

I walked to the door and opened it for him. He lingered there for a moment, and I looked up at him in expectation. "I'm taller than you again," he smiled. "I like it this way."

"Oh? Why? Do you like to feel bigger than a woman? Thinly-veiled misogyny, maybe?"

He winced. "No. Because it's easier for me to do this." He touched the side of his finger to the underside of my chin and tilted it up, then bent slightly to kiss me. My heart skipped a beat as his lips moved slowly over mine. It was a simple, chaste kiss, but there was something so intensely sexy about it I had to hold onto the door for dear life or risk falling to the floor when my knees buckled.

"We're supposed to be friends," I croaked.

"I thought I should practice," he murmured when it ended. "We have to put on a good show next weekend."

When we share a room, I thought, and as I did I realized, it was not horror I felt but anticipation.

41

MIMI

*T*hursday was an odd day for me. Josh kept giving me strangely wounded looks which I completely ignored. I definitely did not want any office gossip to start now that our affair was actually over. Then Tracee came in for the first time since her brother's death, but when I approached her she behaved as if the accident, or her calling me in the middle of the night had never happened. I backed off and let her get on with it.

Everybody else was meeting at a cocktail bar downtown.

"What about you, Mimi? You coming?" Josh asked.

I shook my head and took great pleasure in saying truthfully, "Got a date with Max."

"Oh," he said with a frown.

I left work early and was home well before six. There were so many things I could have done with my time. I could have tossed out all the expired cans from my pantry—and there were more than I felt comfortable admitting to. I could have done laundry—or should have, really. I could have cleaned under my bed. I could have taken the leftovers out of the fridge. I could have even rested so that I would look my best when I went out with Max.

Instead, I paced and tore my brain apart asking all sorts of questions. Why did he kiss me when he did? Why did he take all those opportunities to touch me—my back, my arm, my hand? Was it just to send a message to Josh and everybody else at the party?

Or was it more?

No matter why he'd done it, I couldn't forget how it felt. Electric. It took my breath away. I felt like a little girl with her first crush. Only I wasn't wearing braces and a training bra anymore. Even if I was still as big a dork as I was back then. Ugh, had I really played piano for him? Why didn't I just throw in a few card tricks and show him my rock collection as well?

But he'd asked, hadn't he?

Then I pictured the soft smile on his face and that almost awed look in his eyes and I became confused again.

❄

I opened the door to Max dressed in a black turtleneck sweater and black jeans. Even in a turtleneck, he looked good enough to eat. His gaze roamed over down to my flat ballet slippers, probably my most comfortable shoes besides my sneakers.

"I see you meant what you said last night about going casual."

I motioned to his outfit. "You're not exactly dressed for the

Ritz yourself. Anyway, you said, you liked it when I'm shorter than you."

He grimaced. "If this is what a relationship with you is like, I might have to rethink it."

"Get used to it. You're the one who got us into this." I made a point of lingering behind him to get a look at his butt. Holy hell, he could wear a pair of jeans. I sketched a quick sign of the cross over myself before he could catch me.

We ended up walking a few blocks to a pizza shop with a window that faced the street so customers could order outside or inside. It wasn't too cold out, a good night for walking, so we decided to walk while we ate.

"I can burn calories as I eat them," I joked.

"I told you, you don't need to worry about that," he said, biting into his large slice with extra cheese. A man after my own heart. I could never get enough cheese in my life.

"I do. It's all smoke and mirrors." I grinned before taking a bite of my own slice. It was heaven on a paper plate and almost as big as my head. "I swear, in my next life I'm gonna come back as a cheese shop owner."

He stops walking. "I've seen you naked."

I nearly choke and he has to bang me on my back.

"Thanks," I said with tears in my eyes.

"You all right?"

"I choked and nearly died. I wish you wouldn't say things like that," I grumbled.

He smirked. "Sorry. I couldn't help it. I'm a dick."

He wiped a little tomato sauce from his lips. I couldn't help ogling. That man had lips to die for. We started walking again.

"So is this more your speed?" he asked. "Just some pizza and a walk around town?"

I shrugged. "I can go both ways."

"Provocative." His eyebrows wiggled up and down.

"You know what I mean. God, I have to think about everything I say just in case there's a possible double entendre."

"I never said I had an elevated sense of humor."

"As I was trying to say before I was interrupted by childish humor," I continued pointedly, "I like a nice night out as much as the next person, but I don't need to go all out all the time. Sometimes a girl just wants to wear her flats and eat pizza. And it helps when she has good company."

"I'm flattered."

"I wasn't talking about you."

"Of course not."

42

MIMI

*H*e laughed and we went up and down the street for more than an hour, and I only realized after I got home later on that I never paid attention to exactly where we were. It didn't matter. I was busy talking about my family, how Mom lived on Long Island and Dad had moved to Newark. Max had a million questions, which he chalked up to research.

"I have to know about you," he reminded me. "So we seem legit."

"Tell me more about you," I suggested. "I've talked myself nearly hoarse."

He shrugged, his shoulders moving up and down under his clothes. "There's not that much to tell. Besides the Fields already know everything they need to know about me and are hardly likely to quiz you about it."

"Oof. What a cop out." I laughed.

He looked offended. "It's the truth."

"Liar. You live in a gorgeous apartment in an almost-empty floor. I told you why I haven't left, or at least I think I alluded to it."

"Your grandmother."

"Correct. So, why are you still around?"

He shrugged, looking at the ground. "It's where I live. That's all. I don't want to leave." I liked him even more for that.

I smiled mistily at him. How I wished things were different. "It feels better, knowing I'm not alone. I'm not crazy for sticking around."

He looked into my eyes and shook his head. "No, you're not crazy for sticking around. Not for that."

"You're such a sweet talker. I'll have to make sure everybody knows that when we're in the Hamptons." I put a hand over my heart, fluttering my eyelashes. "And when he told me I was crazy, Mr. Fields, I knew he was the one for me."

He threw back his head and laughed. "And I'll tell them I stay with you even though you're crazy because I feel sorry for you and somebody needs to make sure you take your medicine and wear your panties on the inside of your clothes."

I laughed. "Thanks a lot." I paused. "I know I never really told you this, but I'm really grateful to you."

"For what?"

"For what you did on the street that day with Josh and Lillian. Not many guys would have done that. You're one in a million, Max. You knew I was in trouble and you jumped in. Just like that." I touched his arm. "I never thanked you properly for that. I wanted to hit you at the time, honestly. But I

185

know it was because you felt sorry for me and wanted to help. So...thanks."

"No problem. And I didn't do it because I felt sorry for you. Well, not entirely." He started walking again, and I had no choice but to follow. Who wouldn't?

"Why, then?" I fell in step beside him.

"Because I don't like watching people getting picked on. Your face was as white as a sheet and you looked like you were looking for a way out. I just wanted to get you out of it. So I did."

Underneath his cocky arrogance, he was a sweet guy. "Isn't it ironic then that all you ended up doing was putting me in a position where I was forced to go to their stupid party."

"Yeah, I should have stood there and let you tell them you were having your appendix out."

I giggled. "I don't think that's the sort of surgery you schedule in advance, but you're on the right track."

"Come on." He nudged me a little. "Don't pretend you didn't have a good time."

"It's not on my Top Ten list of best times ever." I was lying. I loved my night with him. Every minute of him pretending to be my adoring boyfriend. And when he kissed my forehead and told me I was the most beautiful woman in that room, he was treating me the way I had dreamed and hoped a man would. Everything he did that night was more than I ever got from Josh or any other man.

"But you enjoyed it," he insisted.

"I enjoyed certain parts of it," I conceded cautiously.

"We got a weekend in the Hamptons out of it."

I snorted. "Don't remind me!"

"Life could be a hell of a lot worse," he reminded. "A weekend in the Hamptons is hardly cause to throw yourself down a flight of stairs."

"Oh, damn. And I was gonna do that as an excuse to get out of it."

I had expected him to laugh, but he frowned, instead. "Am I really that repulsive to you?"

"What kind of crazy talk is that?" I stopped. "I'm just messing with you, Max."

He stopped in front of me, hands in his pockets. I could tell I had upset him.

I touched his arm. "Max, I really didn't mean it that way."

"You have a way of making it sound like you're horrified by the idea. I have to wonder why."

"Not because of you. Never because of you. I mean it. It's because I'm not a good liar, and I would hate to be embarrassed. That's all. I dread the way I know Lillian will look at us. She eyed you up pretty seriously at the party, by the way."

"Did she? I can't imagine why considering who she's engaged to." He rolled his eyes. "Mr. Wonderful himself."

"For a man, you're pretty catty, you know?"

"He hurt you. Why would I like him?"

The thing was, he looked sincere. Like he meant it. But why? He was the son of a rich man. A playboy who had the pick of any woman he wanted. I wasn't anything special. Was it because I said no? What would happen if I said yes?

"Trust me, it's not you I'm worried about." That was true. I was more afraid of myself. I couldn't imagine sharing a bedroom with this man and not wanting to jump his bones.

We kept walking, and he seemed satisfied if not happy with my explanation. "You know, she can't hurt you, right?"

"You didn't read that email from her, Max. You don't know how she really feels about me. Have you ever had somebody call you vile names?"

"More like how many times have I heard it. Words are just words unless you believe them. You don't believe them, do you?"

"At the time? I don't know. I might have."

Max slid an arm around me, and I welcomed the comfort. It felt nice. Very nice. "She seems like a real piece of work," he mused. "And she just found out she was pregnant, so there's that. She went nuts, but it's not your fault. You didn't set out to hurt anybody."

"I know that, but she doesn't."

"That's gotta be enough. It just has to. Sometimes we all do things without thinking about them because we have reasons that make sense to us, but we don't think about the other person. We just make assumptions. Like she assumed you were out to take her man." He made a face. "Although, I can't imagine why anyone would."

I laughed. "Sorry. I hadn't met you yet. I didn't have you to compare him to." I rolled my eyes.

"I'm more than just a pretty face."

"No comment." I blushed to the roots of my hair.

"Watch out!" he exclaimed as he grabbed my arm as I stumbled over a crack in the sidewalk. He kept me from falling, but I turned my ankle and it hurt like a bitch. I laughed because I was embarrassed.

"Are you okay?"

"I'm fine. Just incredibly clumsy." But it did hurt. More than a little. I winced when I put weight on it.

"Hell," he cursed. "You might have sprained it."

"I don't think it's a sprain," I said. "Just soreness."

He hailed a cab. "Come on. Time to get you home."

"Are you serious? I'm okay!" I wanted to die. I wanted to die right then and there. What a loser I was. A clumsy idiot. Give me stilettos and I could walk miles, but put me in a pair of flats and trust me to make a fool of myself.

"You're not okay. I'll feel a lot better when you're home with your ankle elevated. Besides, it's getting late."

"Really. I'm fine. I'll take care of it."

He looked me in the eye. "Why won't you let me take care of you?"

The question left me breathless. "All right," I whispered.

So he helped me into the cab and then up the steps to our building, my arm across his shoulders.

"You'll be okay if you keep it up tonight, with ice on it."

"If you say so, Doc." I could kid all I wanted while he was helping me down the hall, but I couldn't deny that it did hurt.

Like hell. I just didn't want him to know how dangerous I was to myself. It was too embarrassing.

He didn't seem to care as he sat me on the couch, put throw pillows under my sore ankle, then put together an ice pack for me.

"Keep this on," he ordered. "And don't get up unless you absolutely need something."

Just to be safe, he loaded up the coffee table with water, iced tea, the TV remote, my iPad, my phone and a bag of cookies in case I wanted a snack.

"Thank you for being so nice to me," I murmured, a little overwhelmed. "You're my knight all over again."

"Your knight?"

I blushed again. "In shining armor. You know." *Just stop talking, Mimi. Just stop talking.*

He grinned. "My armor's a little tarnished. But I appreciate that."

"I appreciate everything you've done." *Seriously, why are you still talking? Maybe you should've sprained your tongue.*

"We'll see how you feel tomorrow."

Then he kissed the top of my head and left.

"You have everything you need?"

"Mm-hmm. I dropped my bags off with Max last night. He'll have them for me in the car when he picks me up." I checked the time again. Nearly three o'clock. The day had crawled by like a tortoise stuck in drying cement. Or something similarly slow.

"And you've packed for every possible turn of events?" Megan asked.

"I'm not sure how many turns of event you expect. Max says they have a heated pool so I chucked in my best swimsuit. I packed good walking shoes in case that's a thing. My running clothes. Outdoor stuff in the case there, I don't know, sailing…and nice, sedate clothes for dinner."

"What about something for nighttime?"

"I have pajamas."

"I don't mean sleeping."

I was glad she couldn't see my face. "Well, gee, Megan. In that case, I won't need anything, will I?"

"Atta girl!"

"I was being sarcastic."

"What's the point of saying no? You know that's where this is going, so why not just relax and enjoy it?"

I chewed my lip, knowing she was probably right. This was it. The weekend in which we would have sex. It seemed inevitable. The two of us, sharing a room. He would probably smell good like he always did, the jerk. Tempting me. Maybe I'd catch a glimpse of him changing, get a look at his muscular torso and shoulders as he took off his shirt. And my heart would beat faster and the blood would rush to my lady parts and that would be the end of that.

"Hello? You still there?"

"Oh, sure. I'm here."

"Like I said, just enjoy it. Relax and have fun this weekend. What can be more delicious than getting naked with cutie patootie? Oooo…imagine him grabbing you by the hips and slamming into you."

"Megan!" I giggled, my face burning.

"Try getting that mental picture out of your head."

"Ugh, I'm gonna kill you."

"You're welcome and have a great time, okay? Whatever you do don't let the Beast and his Beastess get to you."

"That's gonna be real hard."

"I mean it. Ignore them. Hang on to cutie patootie's arm the whole time. And most important: Keep me in the loop."

"Will do." I was smiling as I hung up. Right, I needed to get the idea of Max's naked body out of my head. He was picking me up in a few minutes, so blushing over the thought of him in all his glorious nakedness wouldn't be helpful.

"Hey."

I swung around in my chair to find Josh standing at the entrance to my cubicle. He was leaning against the wall, hands in his pockets, with a studied air of casualness on his face. I sighed internally. He was the absolute last person I felt like talking to just then.

What did I ever see in him? The question kept perplexing me. Nothing about him seemed attractive to me. I used to think his puppy dog eyes were cute, sort of helpless and sweet. Now I just found them pathetic.

A shame, since he was going all-out to look sheepish and cute. It was really making me want to punch him in the balls since they were at eye level.

Luckily for him, I had to be friendly, or at least civil. We still had to work together, never mind the coming weekend. I guessed that was why he was there. "Ready for the weekend?" I asked brightly.

"Yeah, I'm all packed up. Alexander said we should try to be there by six, right?"

I nodded. Of course, I knew that as I had received the same email from Alexander telling us traffic going out on a Friday got crazy from five to seven o'clock. He suggested leaving early ("just this once, ha ha ha") to get there before the roads jammed up.

"Have you ever been there?" I asked.

He shook his head. "I have no idea what to expect."

"I thought you ran in those circles all the time," I said. It was easy to fall back into my old role of supporting him and making him feel better. When we were just talking like two normal people, I could pretend the humiliation he'd put me through hadn't happened. I could pretend he hadn't lied to me and made me look like a trollop. I could pretend he wasn't a spineless liar.

"My parents do. Sure, I've been out to the Hamptons before, but it's not really my scene. It's more Lill's thing than mine."

I almost gagged at his use of her nickname. Lill. Why did he have to go and mention her name? Like I wouldn't see enough of her over the weekend. Like her very presence wasn't enough to make me wish I could sink into the floor-boards and never come back. I'd already had nightmares about her cornering me at the house and tearing into me— literally, with claws and everything. I'd seen the blood and fire in her eyes as she accused me of everything from stealing her man to causing the housing crisis back in 2009. I mean everything.

I faked a merry laugh. "Then I guess it'll be your thing soon, huh?"

His face changed when I joked like that, and I remembered him looking the same way when Max joked along similar lines at the party.

"Lill will make a good wife," he said defensively.

I pitied him then. Max's explanation at the party had cast the whole ugly thing in a different light. There was no excuse for cheating, ever, but when I saw it as evidence of his weakness

it softened the blow. I couldn't hate somebody I could identify with. I was not perfect.

"I'm sure she will. Good luck to you."

He nodded and shifted his position.

"What's there to do out there?" I asked since he didn't seem
to be ready to leave my cubicle. I did make it a point to start
wrapping it up, though, packing up my laptop and locking
my drawers.

"Oh, you know, the usual stuff."

I had to laugh. "No, I don't know. Hello? Remember who
you're talking to here."

He chuckled. "Right. Sorry. Uh, I think Alexander has a sail-
boat. I know they have a heated saltwater pool and a hot tub.
Tennis, but it's probably too cool out for that. I think their
property includes hiking trails, too."

"Sounds nice. I'm sure we'll have a good time." Oh, I was such
a liar. Such a terrible, dreadful liar. If he knew, he didn't seem
to care. He was probably relieved I wasn't crying and threat-
ening grievous bodily harm after he crushed my hopes for
our happy life together. Or something like that.

Why wasn't he walking away?

Why didn't he get the hint?

In his next breath, he explained what he was really doing
there. "I've been meaning to ask you something. I hope you
don't take it the wrong way."

"Ooh, mysterious," I chuckled.

"It's just...I mean..." He looked around, making sure we
weren't overheard. Tracee was hard at work in her office,

probably wondering why she didn't get an invite to the Hamptons. "Well, I thought you and I were a thing."

I blinked once, twice. When I realized he wasn't going to keep talking, I prompted him. "And?"

"And I guess I was just wondering, well..."

Suddenly, I knew exactly what he was going to ask.

MIMI

"*I* was just wondering...when Max came into the picture?"

I wanted to be the bigger person. I really, truly did. I even tried folding my arms and sternly telling myself I had to control my temper. It wouldn't do any good to claw his eyes out, especially not in the middle of the office where there were so many witnesses.

But sadly, there was no holding back a hurricane. You just had to let it rip before it moved on.

"You thought we were a thing? Is that what you thought?" I asked calmly. (Yes, that was the calm before the storm.)

"Of course. We were great together, weren't we?"

"That's good to know, since it looked to me you were just screwing me behind your girlfriend's back," I snarled.

His eyes went wide, his mouth dropped open. "Don't get mad," he said and held up his hands, trying to shush me. I would not be shushed. The time for shushing was over.

Unruly Mimi had come out, rearing her head, and I wasn't about to make her shut up.

"Don't get mad?" I growled.

"We agreed it's all water under the bridge. I just wanted to know when you started seeing him, that's all."

"It's none of your business when he came into my life," I spat, and my blood boiled at his audacity. "I can't believe you, Josh. Where do you get off?"

"Okay, okay. You're right." His head whipped from side to side so fast, I was sure he'd need a neck brace. "I shouldn't have asked. Just drop it."

"Yeah, I'll just drop it the way you just dropped me." I gathered my things together, still beyond furious. As I put on my coat and slung my purse and laptop bag over my shoulder, I muttered, "Come into my cubicle and ask me questions about my private life when he's the one who screwed me over. What the hell is wrong with him? I swear to God..."

"I'm still standing right here, you know."

"Well, maybe you'd better do something about that."

"Yeah. I'll leave you alone now." Just as I thought he was about to turn around and leave, he stopped. "I hope you'll be able to forget about this by the time we get out there. We need to put up a united front."

My eyebrows flew upwards. Honestly, this man was incredible. "Why? Don't you want him to know he's invited a filthy cheater to his home for the weekend? What would his wife think?" I couldn't believe I was being so nasty. I was never that nasty, but then I had never faced the sort of situation he'd put me in. I guess I was turning over a new leaf. A rather vicious, potentially violent leaf.

"Please, Mims."

I wanted to kick him. "Don't call me that."

His eyes widened, pleading with me. "Please, Mimi. Don't make a thing out of this."

I drew a long, shaky breath. "Josh, if you'll remember, I was just fine before you raked the past up. I was actually stupid enough for a second there to believe we could be friendly without letting what happened get in between us. But you had to open your stupid mouth. Way to go. If things go sour this weekend, it won't be my fault."

Since he stood there gaping like a fish and wouldn't get out of my way, I pushed past him with my shoulder. I could barely see thanks to the tears of rage welling up in my eyes, but I managed to make it down the hall to the elevators without stumbling into anybody or anything. Always a plus.

I couldn't go out to face Max feeling the way I was, though. He'd know right away there was something wrong with me. So I went to the ladies' room in the lobby and texted Megan.

Run-in with Josh. Finally asked when Max came into the picture. Completely unrelated: Do you think anybody would suspect me if he mysteriously disappears this weekend?

It took her all of twenty seconds to reply.

Be sure to fill his pockets with rocks. It'll help weigh down the body.

She could make me laugh even when I felt like a total wreck.

Leave it to Josh to get inside my head just before I had to leave for a stressful weekend. I splashed my cheeks with cold water and fixed my makeup, taking deep breaths as I did. Josh was nothing. He couldn't get to me. I just had to stop focusing on how much I couldn't stand him and take our interaction back to the professional relationship we once had. I was not giving up my job because of him. Why should I?

My phone buzzed again, only this time it wasn't Megan.

Your chariot awaits. Do I have to come up there and get you?

Oh, Jesus, no. Not that.

Waiting for the elevator. Be down in a sec.

As much fun as it would be to watch him and Josh go head-to-head one more time before we had to be civilized in front of grownups, I didn't want to press my luck. He didn't need to know I was cowering in a bathroom, either. Which, in the end, was exactly what I was doing. I was cowering and telling myself I didn't have it in me to hold my head up.

And that just wasn't true.

"You can do this," I whispered to myself in the mirror. "You can go out there and pretend that hot, sexy guy in the sports car—and I don't know what he drives, but I bet it's a sports car—is your boyfriend. Your hot, sexy boyfriend who adores you and would never use you while cheating on another woman. You can pretend you adore him because let's face it, you're already pretty close to doing that. There are much worse problems in life than pretending to have a sexy boyfriend while spending a weekend in the Hamptons."

"You're right," said a phantom voice in one of the stalls. I jumped a mile and fell against the paper towel dispenser.

"Stop whining and get the hell out of here so I can use the bathroom in peace."

"Sorry, sorry." I scrambled to get my things together and hurled myself through the door into the lobby, then out the main doors before I lost my momentum.

Sure enough, he was waiting for me beside a shiny red sex machine, low slung and practically purring. It gleamed in the mid-afternoon sun, and even the fancy bigshots in their expensive suits paused to take a look as they walked by. If Max were a car, he would be that very car. I imagined draping myself across it the way they did in music videos.

He looked pretty awesome too, but then he always did. He'd gone all-out with the 'Weekend in the Hamptons' look— khakis, a pale blue button-down, dark blue blazer, loafers. I made an 'ok' sign with my thumb and forefinger.

"You approve?" he asked.

"If I didn't know any better, I'd think you walked out of an ad in *Town & Country*." I held my arms out to my sides. "What about me?"

Dark sunglasses concealed his eyes, but his smile told me I passed muster. "You could wear a potato sack and you'd still get my pulse racing."

"Are you sure you should be driving when you're clearly under the influence of a controlled substance?"

He laughed. "And I thought you'd gotten better at taking a compliment."

"I must have regressed."

He stepped away from the car, taking my laptop bag and putting it in the trunk—my things were already inside, as promised. "Ready for some fun?" he asked, opening the passenger door with a wicked grin.

I gulped, wondering exactly what he meant by 'fun'. I guess I'd find out soon enough.

"*Y*ou've got to be kidding me. Oh, my flipping God," I exclaimed as we rolled up on the Fields estate around five-thirty, just as the light in the sky started to fade. The house was lit up, light gleaming from each and every window. And there were a lot of windows. It was a lot of house.

"Do you think they have somebody on staff whose job it is to turn on all the lights at night?" I asked in wonder.

Max chuckled as he put the car in park and turned off the engine. "They're probably on a timer," he offered. "Or they're lit for guests, to wow them when they first pull up."

"It worked," I breathed.

"I see it did."

How could I help sitting there with my mouth hanging open? It was like something out of a movie. The driveway, if it could even be called that, was stone paved and ended in a circle in front of the massive three-story mansion. A fountain bubbled in the center of the circle, beyond which sat the garage. I wondered how many cars it held.

The house itself wasn't imposing even with its size. Whoever had designed it kept comfort and hominess in mind, I thought. It was more like an oversized farmhouse than a chateau. I counted four chimneys extending up from the roof, and wraparound porches on all three levels. I wondered what it would be like to sit out there at night with a glass of wine or hot cocoa, breathing in the smell of money. Because oh, boy, did it smell like money around here. Money and cashmere and Egyptian cotton. And there I was, plain little old me, in the center of it.

"You should see the back," Max grinned as he got out of the car. I guessed that meant I had to get out, too.

"Even better?" I asked, standing on cramped legs. The car was sexy but even with fine leather seats, it was uncomfortable going. Two hours left me stiff. Small price to pay, I decided.

"Just wait and see."

"Okay."

"It's a shame we're not out here in the summer."

I wondered just how much time he'd spent out here if Fields was only his parents' friend and advisor. Then again, that was what people in his circle did. That was the whole reason I was out here because Alexander had a habit of randomly inviting people out for the weekend. If I ever got rich, like really rich, I would do the same thing.

The house gleamed like a jewel against the darkening sky, and inside I could see high ceilings and large, airy rooms. A wide, short staircase led up to the front door. Max took my hand to lead the way.

"What about our things?"

"Somebody will be out to get them," he promised. "Just relax and enjoy."

I decided to keep my mouth shut and stop giving away the fact that I was a total newbie to the Hamptons experience as Max rang the bell.

A maid answered, smiling warmly as she greeted us. "Mr. and Mrs. Fields are in the great room," she said, gesturing to her left.

Max walked confidently in that direction. I could hear soft music playing, and the sounds of laughter as our feet clicked on the polished wood floor.

"Is that Maximus?" Millicent Fields asked, hurrying over to us, arms extended. "I haven't seen you in, what, since Christmas?" She instantly struck me as a very lovely person. She had a genuine, radiant smile and gave him an actual kiss on the cheek versus an air kiss. I'd only ever seen her at company functions, looking regal and demure, but in her home, she was the image of graciousness and warmth.

"And you look as lovely as ever," Max said suavely, giving her a hug.

She ran a hand over her ice-blonde hair as if smoothing it back into place and smiled at him affectionately. Then she turned to me and pursed her lips, thinking. "I'm sure I've seen you before. We bumped into each other at the buffet table during the last holiday party, didn't we?"

I laughed, realizing she was right. "And I almost made you spill your chateaubriand all over your beautiful dress."

"But you didn't," she chuckled. "Mimi, right?"

"Yes."

Alexander stood behind a bar at the other end of the room, mixing cocktails by a blazing fire. "Come on, you two. Let's get you fixed up with some drinks." Millicent went to him, while Max and I followed behind her.

"You're doing amazing," Max whispered.

"I can't believe she knew!"

"She's like that. Remembers everything. Mind like a steel trap." Max smiled as he shook Alexander's hand, and I did the same.

It was bizarre, standing there in my boss's house. And what a house. The 'great room', as the maid called it, was roughly the size of a basketball court. It was two stories, with a series of windows along the back wall stretching from floor to ceiling. I caught a glimpse of a pool and hot tub, just as Josh had mentioned, and beyond that was an expanse of water.

Still, in spite of its size, it was a cozy room, comfortably furnished.

I decided I liked Millicent's taste in décor. Some people would have crammed antiques and paintings and other la-de-dah things in there, but not her. Overstuffed couches in cream and blue, plenty of pillows and throw blankets, flowers, and candles. I could imagine curling up by the fire with a good book.

"You're the first to arrive," our host informed us.

"Are you expecting many people this weekend?" Max asked.

"Josh Williams, his fiancée and her parents," Alexander replied. "It should be a great weekend."

My stomach dropped. Lillian's parents, too? I prayed they didn't know who I was.

Millicent winked at me. "My husband has the habit of inviting all sorts of people out here at once. I wasn't able to attend the engagement party last weekend, but when he came home, he informed me it would be a full house."

"I hope that's all right," I murmured, alarmed and unsure what else to say.

"Oh, don't get me wrong. If I didn't love to entertain, I wouldn't have a home like this." Her voice dropped to a whisper. "But I'm sure you'd rather not hang out with a bunch of old people this weekend. He doesn't take things like that into account."

I smiled and shook my head. "It's a real pleasure being here with you. I was thrilled to be invited. You have such a beautiful home."

"Thank you, sweetheart. We're very lucky." Out of anybody else's mouth, that would have come off like the most pathetic humblebrag ever. But from her, it sounded sincere. I liked her so darn much. She wasn't the stereotypical dry, upper-crust WASP. I felt like we could sit and gossip like girlfriends.

"What are you two talking about?" my boss asked before handing me a glass of straw-colored wine.

"I was telling Mrs. Fields how lovely I think your home is," I explained. "Thank you for inviting me."

"Of course, dear, of course." He still looked like he had no idea who I was or why I was there. I chalked that up to him being an exuberant host. He tossed out invitations like he was giving out candy, without taking account of who he'd invited.

The doorbell rang, and Max took my hand. Whether he did it to make me feel better or to carry out the whole 'we're so in love' thing, I didn't know. Not that it even mattered. I was so grateful for him just then, even if he had gotten me into the mess I was in.

"Hello, hello!" Lillian rushed over to Millicent, and the two of them gushed together about how nice it was to see each other. I did a quick once-over of the glowing mother-to-be in her skinny jeans and baggy sweater. Once again, she looked painstakingly casual. It was a gift, I was sure, looking so hip and so carefree at the same time. Like she'd just thrown her outfit together while piling her golden hair in a messy bun on top of her head.

Her leather riding boots and the Birkin bag over one arm might have made me murderously jealous for a second or two, but my jealousy was tempered by the fact that she had to carry Josh's little brat to full term, deliver it and bring it up. No bag or shoe could make up for that kind of crap on a cracker.

Josh nodded at me then made small talk with Alexander and Lillian's parents, Peter and Gretchen, who remembered me from the engagement party and smiled tightly at me. They were much more like what I'd expected Millicent to be like. I hoped we wouldn't have to spend too much time together.

Max must have sensed my hesitation. He slid an arm around my waist, leaning in as if nuzzling me. "You're doing great," he whispered.

"Good thing, since we've been here for maybe fifteen minutes," I whispered back.

His breath stirred the hair at the nape of my neck as he chuckled, and I shivered with sudden goosebumps.

"We could always spend the weekend in our room if that makes you feel any better," he murmured, his hand tightening around my waist.

"And what would we do there? Play chess?"

"Of course. That's all I brought with me. Clean underwear and my chess set."

I giggled. "You'll have to teach me."

"Oh, don't worry. I'll teach you."

I felt my skin reddening. "Are you a good teacher?"

"I believe in repetition. Over and over until you get it right. I mean, we do have all weekend."

I was glad Millicent interrupted us since I wasn't sure if I could continue our conversation without turning myself on right there in front of my boss and his guests. I'd never spent a weekend in the Hamptons, but I was willing to bet that wasn't considered good form.

"Now that we're all here, I'll let the chef know to get dinner finished. If you'd like to go upstairs and get settled, I'll call you down when we're ready to eat."

Oh. Upstairs. The one place I simultaneously most and least wanted to be.

46

MIMI

The maid showed us to our room, which sat at the top of a wide, curving staircase and directly to the left. Several other doors lined the long hallway, all closed. She opened our door, and my heart pounded so hard I almost couldn't hear over the blood rushing in my ears.

Our bedroom.

For the whole weekend.

Well, we had more than enough space—roughly the size of my entire apartment. No wonder Max thought my place was small. A four-poster bed sat against one wall. I couldn't look at it without blushing. There was a chaise lounge by the window. I wondered if Max would do the gentlemanly thing and offer to spend the night in it, or do the caveman thing and demand to share the bed. I almost hoped he'd demand.

Okay, I did more than *almost* hope.

I ran my hand over the beautiful antique dresser, then examined the lovely little vanity and velvet padded stool. The room was decorated in shades of cream and light gray, with touches of yellow here and there which brightened up all the dark wood in the floors and furniture. It reminded me of an English country hotel. I couldn't imagine having entire rooms like that one, all set up just in case guests visited. I'd sleep in a different room each night just to say I got some use out of them.

Our bags had been placed along the wall, just as Max said they would.

"It's unnerving," I said, shaking my head.

"What is?"

"Having servants walking around, doing things while you're enjoying the wine and the fire."

He had started unpacking, pulling out socks and underwear. He stopped and looked at me strangely. "It's not slavery, you know. They get paid very well for what they do. They chose this profession. Just like you chose yours."

"Okay. Don't bite my head off."

"Then stop being such an inverted snob and pretending there is an insurmountable mountain of difference between you and me."

"Hey, I didn't mean to offend you."

"You didn't. I just think you will enjoy your weekend better without that chip on your shoulder."

I bit my lip. He was right. Both Alexander and Millicent had shown me nothing but genuine hospitality. I should stop feeling so insecure and just have fun. "Hey. We didn't talk about which drawers go to which person."

He frowned. "There's an entire chest of drawers here. We can split them up three and three."

"I wanted the top drawers."

"Why?"

"Just because," I said airily.

"You're so strange." But he let me have my way, taking the fourth drawer and working his way down. Then he glanced up at me. "Aren't you unpacking?"

I shifted my weight from one foot to the other. "I'll wait my turn."

He straightened up. "Why wait?"

"You can get the shit-eating grin off your face anytime you want," I said, folding my arms.

"Are you afraid I'll see your panties and lose all control?" he asked, taking one slow step toward me, then another.

"No." Yes.

"Or do you want to make sure I don't catch a glimpse of your sexy underwear?" He kept walking toward me, making me back away until he had me up against the bed.

"I'm just afraid you couldn't handle it," I quipped. "Your poor heart might not be able to take all the excitement." My false bravado slipped when I realized there was nowhere for me to go. I feinted left, then right, trying to get around him—but he was too fast for me. I squealed as he threw his arms around me, pinning my arms to my sides. We both laughed and fell onto the bed.

He was right there, so close to me, and we were both horizontal. On a bed. I stopped laughing. So did he.

"I can take the chaise longue if you want."

"Do you want to?" *Please say no. Please say no. Please kiss me right now and say no.*

One corner of his mouth curled upward as his eyes fixed on mine. "Do you want me to?"

I shook my head slowly. "Not when there's all this bed to enjoy. But only if you think you can handle being so close to all this." I waved my hands over my body.

He growled, setting my heart racing again. "I can barely handle it right now. What do you think it'll be like later on?"

I would have answered, but I stopped breathing and I needed to be able to breathe if I wanted to speak.

"Dinner's ready!" someone called from outside the door.

He groaned, and I laughed as the moment dissolved. What would have happened if one of the staff hadn't made her announcement? I knew what would have happened. I was an adult, and it was time to stop pretending there was nothing between us. That our appearance that weekend was all fake because it wasn't. I wasn't nearly as unhappy to be there as I had pretended to be.

"So much for timing," he muttered, rolling away from me.

Oh, boy. There was no missing the telltale bulge in his khakis. In a parallel universe I would be passing up on dinner and living on lovin', but in my little world that would be rude and stupid. Though it would send a clear message to Josh, which would have almost made it worthwhile.

The thought of Josh reminded me of something important. I got up quickly, sex the last thing on my mind. All right, maybe not the last, but not the first anymore. "We have to get our stories straight."

"On what?" Max sat up, still looking flustered and put out at being interrupted.

"On when and how we met." I gave him a very brief, very abridged version of the run-in with Josh. "He asked when you came into the picture."

"It's none of his business."

"Yes, well, I still think we should agree on a time when we started dating. Somebody's bound to ask just to make small talk," I pointed out.

"I don't think there's anything wrong with saying we've known each other for a long time but didn't start officially dating until a few weeks ago."

"Works for me." As long as it didn't look like I was being just as slimy as Josh was.

47

MIMI

As it turned out, I had no reason to worry that night. Lillian's wedding plans and questions about her unexpected pregnancy dominated the conversation at the dinner table, with her mother and Millicent asking question after question. I had nothing to contribute to the conversation, so I stayed silent.

The men had their talk, too, all about football—college and pro. I was just as lost there, too. And so was Josh, from what I could tell. While Max laughed and joked with the other men about their teams—it seemed like his team was doing better than theirs, though I couldn't keep track of all the names they dropped—Josh stayed quiet. I wondered what was bothering him, but it was a vague question in the back of my mind.

Maybe it was the way Max rarely stopped touching me—his hand on my knee, occasionally picking up my hand to kiss the back of it. He'd lean in to kiss my cheek every so often, or rest his hand on the back of my neck. Even though I wasn't part of his conversation, I was always on his mind.

And I. Ate. It. Up.

Was I being smug? Eh, maybe a little, but it wasn't every day when I had the most handsome man at the table all over me. I'd have to write a letter to Santa and tell him I'd understand if he didn't bring me anything that year. Christmas had come early.

"I think the two of you are just adorable," Millicent murmured with a warm smile. She sat at the foot of the table, with me on her right. From the corner of my eye, I could see Lillian turn to stare at me. The spotlight was finally off her and she didn't like it one bit.

"Thanks. He's just too much, isn't he?" I deliberately gushed.

She gave Max a fond look. "It's so nice to see him looking happy for once. I'm glad he finally found the right girl."

Wow, somebody up there was trying to tempt me, weren't they? I glanced over at Max, who was deep in conversation about the playoffs, then leaned in to whisper to Millicent "What's the story there?"

"Oh, you know men like him. Too busy to settle down." She laughed it off, then went back to her conversation about flower arrangements or place settings or whatever the new topic was. My eyes fell on Lillian as I turned back to my food. She could try to hide how irritated the sight of Max and me made her, but she was a pretty poor actress. I didn't let her know I noticed her, but wrapped an arm around Max's ridiculously thick bicep and kissed his smooth-shaven cheek. I was already having a lot more fun than I ever imagined.

"*I* thought they'd never let us go to bed," Max said when we finally reached the bedroom.

We'd sat around the table for three solid hours, then spent another two hours by the fire over drinks and decaf and even more talk of the 'Wedding of the Year'. I felt like I had already attended it, only I didn't even have a party favor to take home with me.

I had caught myself yawning more than once, then started biting the side of my tongue to keep from offending anyone when a yawn sneaked up on me.

I sat on the bed with a heavy sigh, tired in my bones. "No offense to them, but I thought older people went to bed earlier. Maybe I'm an old lady in a young woman's body."

"Yeah, ya are." He smirked at me from the closet, where he was hanging up his blazer.

"I've been in these shoes all day," I murmured, kicking them off.

"You and shoes," he chuckled.

"Stop being a pain in the ass."

He walked over to where I sat. A slow burn started in my toes and started working its way up my legs. I held my breath. What was he going to do? I watched, waiting, my heart racing so fast I thought it would explode. He had to hear it racing. How did he not hear it racing? I was surprised people in other rooms couldn't hear it.

When he sank to his knees, I couldn't believe my eyes. Gently, he took one of my feet in his hands and, without saying a word, started massaging it. I prayed like I had never prayed before that it wasn't sweaty, or worse, smelly. Talk about a mood killer. I watched him like a hawk, but he didn't recoil in horror, or throw up in his mouth. So I figured I was good.

And so was he. Oh, was he ever good at a foot massage. "Do you work part-time in a spa or something?" I whispered, closing my eyes.

"No," he murmured with a laugh.

"A massage parlor?"

"Not for a long time. I got tired of the happy ending stuff."

I giggled, even as fire blazed and crackled in my core. He sparked something deep inside me, something I didn't want to ignore any longer.

I let out a soft moan, and when he looked up and our eyes locked, I curled and uncurled one finger. Beckoning, inviting, wanting.

He knelt between my legs, hands sliding up my legs as he straightened up. I wrapped my legs around him, pulling him in closer while winding my arms around his neck. My nostrils filled with the scent of aftershave and soap and that heady smell that was Max. Was it really happening? Were we going to take that big leap together?

Yes.

48

MIMI

I opened my mouth to say something, no doubt something stupid, so it was a good thing that the man moved forward and covered it with a soul-searing kiss. It was so raw with brutal need that I just about managed to cling to his hard shoulders. My tongue was caught, stroked, and pulled into the warm cave of his mouth and sucked.

The fire exploded into an inferno.

I feasted my eyes and hands and mouth on his body, exploring him as he worshiped me. It was like a dream coming true—total, all-consuming passion. He laid a hand gently on my cheek and tenderly, very tenderly, as if I was the most precious and delicate thing in the world, brushed his fingers down my neck. That was it for me. I gave myself over to him completely.

He kissed the hollow of my throat and tips of my breasts, he stroked my hair, he caressed my back, he nibbled my ear, he licked my belly button. He drove me crazy. God, I wanted him so damn much I wanted to beg him to enter me. I looked at him, my hands on his shoulders, my legs around his waist.

He thrust his tongue into my mouth and withdrew it. Then he did it again. And again. He was fucking my mouth with his tongue. It was a rehearsal for what was about to happen between my legs. It was so dirty and so hot. The harder and faster he did it the more desperate I grew for him. The effect was so profound my hips were practically bucking in tandem with his thrusting. He lifted my dress and looked at the way my wet panties clung to my shape. I felt myself blush.

He looked up and met my eyes. "Are you okay? You ready for this?"

I could tell he was straining, struggling to hold back. He wanted to go ahead, desperately—he shook all over—but he wanted to be sure I was ready and good to go. That one little thing, the way he held back to be sure I was ready, took me from liking him to something much deeper.

Oh, sweet Jesus. I'm in love with him.

"Yes," I breathed, nodding.

My brain vaguely processed the sound of zipper metal teeth grinding down. My dress fell away from my shoulders and he pushed it down to my hips. My body melted another few degrees and searing heat bloomed between my legs. He unhooked my bra and my breasts swung free. He pushed me gently back onto the bed and dragged my dress down my hips and pulled it clean off me. I lay before him, on display, every inch of me offered up to his eyes. He could have done anything with me.

He slipped his fingers into the waistband of my panties and with aching slowness pulled them down my legs. Then he placed his hands on my thighs, opened them wide, and stared at my exposed, aroused sex.

"I've never seen a pussy that begged to be sucked like yours does," he said. "Fuck, I could suck you all day and all night."

My breath hitched at the expression in his eyes. They glittered with triumph. Like a man who was looking down with satisfaction at what he owned.

"I'm going to spend the whole night doing things to your body that you never even dreamed were possible," he said with a dark laugh and stood.

I watched him undress and not once did he take his eyes off me and my open sex.

I don't swear a lot, but by God, naked, he was fucking gorgeous.

He had a tattoo of an eagle on his left bicep. My fingertips itched to trace the intricate blue lines. I let my eyes run down his smooth abs to that holy hell massive cock of his. He was so big and hard, the angry veins twisting up it looked like they were swollen to bursting. I watched wide-eyed as he bent down to kneel between my legs.

My heart was beating so hard I could hear the blood rushing in my ears.

He slipped his hands under my buttocks so that I was open to him like a platter of food. He brought his face close to my pussy and inhaled me deeply. "I love the taste of your wet cunt, Mimi. I've been dreaming of this ever since I had my first taste that night. But you had to run off like a little rabbit before I could finish the job."

I gazed at him with dazed eyes as his tongue moved slowly between my glistening lips and I moaned with excitement.

"Oh God," I moaned and shivered.

"I'm never going to get enough of you, Mimi Young," he growled as he began to feast on my pussy. His greed was obscene and dirty and awesome. No one had even eaten me so hungrily. Josh liked to eat pussy, but never like this. My hips pressed against his face and my hands clenched around his head and pulled him in. I wanted more. I couldn't get enough. My breath came in quick sharp gasps.

"I don't want to wait anymore," I cried hoarsely, and shamelessly tried to open my legs wider for him. I knew what his cock felt like at the entrance of my pussy. I wanted it inside. All of it. Every beautiful inch.

But all he did was push a finger into me and lazily dip it in and out of me.

My head began to buzz as intense pleasure radiated from my core. Then a massive climax the likes of which I had never experienced began to rip right through me. I lost control. I felt as if I was exploding into white spots of ecstasy. I didn't even realize that I had opened my mouth to scream my head off until Max's large hand slapped over my mouth.

"Shhh…baby. Shhhh," he said.

While my muscles were still convulsing and throbbing he took his hand off my mouth and pushed a long, thick finger inside my pulsating sex.

"Oh, God," I groaned, as my pussy clenched his finger.

He pulled his finger out and brought it to my lips. "Suck," he ordered.

I opened my mouth and sucked my own juices off his finger.

He smiled at the sight.

Then he pulled the finger from my mouth and plunged it into me again. When my mouth opened in a gasp, he removed his finger and made me suck it again. Watching me like a hawk as he thrust that finger in and out and back into my mouth. In and out and back in my mouth. He was making me eat my own pussy. It was filthy and a huge turn-on.

Suddenly, I knew what I wanted to taste next. "I want to suck your cock," I said.

He smiled slowly. "I've been wanting to hear you say that from the day I saw you at the elevator."

He always wanted me! That was crazy! The cables of the lift I was traveling in just snapped. I was freefalling. I got on my hands and knees and as I came closer I inhaled the manly smell of him and it made me almost dizzy with excitement and anticipation. I licked the satiny-soft skin on the head of his cock. The pearl of cum at the tip of it dissolved on my tongue. I liked his taste. I really did. It wasn't stale and bitter, but salty and fresh. Like the ocean. I licked him again.

"Oh fuck," he groaned.

Then I stretched my mouth to accommodate his girth. He felt large and heavy on my tongue as my lips closed in on his shaft. My tongue slid around the shape of his swollen head and his hands fisted my hair.

"Fuck, Mimi. That feels amazing," he groaned as he guided my face forward and forced my mouth to take more of him.

I sucked him with deep drawing pulls as his hips moved

forward and back. Just as I was getting into my groove he pulled out with a wet pop.

I looked at him in surprise. I truly wanted to satisfy him, return the pleasure he had given me. "What's wrong?"

"On your back, baby. The wait is over," he said. His voice was thick and guttural. He picked up a foil packet from the bedside table and tore it open.

I lay back and watched him roll the condom over his massive cock and put his knee on the bed. Then those strong powerful thighs spread me wide open. He positioned his cock at my entrance and pushed in. The thick head entered me and my flesh opened like butter to accommodate him.

Hot damn, my eyes widened with shock at how big he was, at the sensation of being so stretched. My mouth opened in a soundless cry of pleasure. "Oh, my God, I'm so full. I've never been this full before."

He paused and gave me time to adjust to the thick, deep intrusion before he began to thrust again. Hard. I gasped with the sensation of being so incredibly stretched. He was so thick and solid. I looked at his beautiful face and a thrill of pleasure fizzled right through me. Max Black and I were doing it. I loved our bodies being joined, his chest crushing down on my breasts, and his hard body pressing down on mine.

My fingers gripped his thick shoulder then slid down the lean muscles of his body to his tight butt as it flexed while he pumped in and out. Every time he buried his cock deep in me I groaned. Never had I felt anything like that with anyone else. Ever. The pleasure was so strong the rest of the world stopped existing. I forgot where I was. I felt my core muscles start clenching as I started to climax. I don't know whether I would have screamed, but Max locked his mouth onto mine. The kiss was hard and demanding and fiery. I walked over the edge into the abyss of pleasure while sucking his tongue blindly and his cock thrusting so hard my body was jerking and sliding on the bed. From somewhere far away I heard him call my name. And it was beautiful.

*I*t was barely light outside when I woke up in Max's arms. Yep, it was a pretty good place to be, all things considered. He spooned me, and I was glad for that —nobody wanted to wake up the first morning after sleeping with somebody knowing their morning breath was hitting their partner right in the face. I was also betting that I'd drooled in my sleep or at least snored a little. Because there was no way life was really as perfect as it seemed just then. Something had to be wrong.

I ran that hand over my face. No dried drool. There was a chance I wouldn't scare him away, after all.

Last night seemed like a dream. A dirty, erotic, incredibly beautiful dream. But it must have been real, or else why would I still be buck naked and so sore between my legs, the kind of soreness a woman felt after having sex three times in one night? And why would he be lying just as naked with his arm over me? I heard his soft, even breathing behind me and relished the sound.

I was in love. No doubt about it. Only a woman in love could find the sound of her lover's breathing so joyful and fulfilling.

I only wished I knew how he felt about me.

Don't overthink this, Mimi. That never got you anywhere. The only thing overthinking ever got me was chewed-up finger-nails and the very real concern of developing an ulcer. Besides, thinking too much made a girl do stupid things like become jealous, clingy, and possessive. I didn't want to be any of those things. I wanted us to be us, just the way we were. If I read too much into it, I'd make it weird even if I tried not to.

He stirred, letting out a confused snort as he did. I stifled a giggle.

"Good morning," he murmured, pulling me close.

Oh, he felt so good. His body was warm and firm as he enveloped me. I let myself sink into the sensation of his lips against the back of my neck, my throat, my ear, my jaw. He wasn't trying to be sexy, but it didn't matter. I felt my body respond like he'd flipped a switch.

"You're up early," I whispered. I took a chance and rolled over, hoping I didn't look like something out of a haunted house. Damn him for looking even more delicious first thing in the morning than he did all day long. How was that even possible? Did he wake up in the middle of the night to make himself look presentable? Even his hair looked artfully tousled. Like he had a hair and makeup crew in that suitcase of his.

"Didn't you hear me making plans to go fishing with Alexander and Peter this morning?"

I frowned. "I guess I missed it. Was that before or after you started placing bets on this year's football draft?"

He chuckled softly. "After."

"I see."

"You could come, you know."

I wrinkled my nose before I could stop myself. "I don't think that would be the best idea. The thought of hooking a fish turns my stomach a little."

"Do you eat fish?"

"Like it's my job, but that's another story."

"Hypocrite." He kissed my forehead, my cheeks. It was heaven. I wished time would stop. Everything was perfect, right here in our cocoon.

"That's not hypocritical. It's me, having a weak stomach. Besides," I added, snuggling up against him just a little closer, "you need your guy time. I would only ruin it."

"I don't think you could ruin anything." He stroked my face, my hair, before letting his hand move down to my back. I told myself to stop shivering every time he touched me, but I couldn't help it. He was magic.

"I wish I could see myself the way you do," I admitted, closing my eyes as his lips found mine.

"I wish you could, too. I really do." He held my chin in his hand, then kissed me again before getting up. "I guess I'd better do this now, or else I might never leave." He looked down at me in all his glorious nakedness, and I let my eyes linger on his body as long as I could.

"I'm taking a mental picture," I told him, then held my hands up on either side of my face like I was holding a camera.

"Wow, is that supposed to be an actual camera in your hands? And you accuse me of dating myself."

"Oh, sorry. Should it be a phone, instead?"

"Yeah. Try living in this century." I threw a pillow at him and he laughed as he stepped into our bathroom.

Just before he closed the door, I murmured, "And to think. I was going to suggest we take a shower together this morning."

The door stopped moving. "Uh, we can definitely still do that."

"Why would you want to take a shower with a woman who doesn't even live in this century?"

I rolled over, giggling to myself with my back to the door. So I didn't see him rush to the bed, but I did feel him scoop me up in his arms and carry me to the shower. I could have fought him off, but why bother? He was a man who got what he wanted.

And he wanted me.

*W*hy I needed her cunt so much was a fucking mystery to me. With every other woman, I immediately lost a big chunk of my desire for her the second I finished I fucking her. And every time we fucked I lost more and more until I couldn't even bear to be in the same room as her. But not with Mimi. With her, I couldn't get enough. Fucking her was like pouring oil on fire. Just made the flames rise higher.

The more I got the more I wanted.

I put her on her feet and she gazed at my cock. I stood still and allowed her. When her gaze left my erect cock, and rose up to meet my eyes, I stepped into the shower and pulled her with me. I turned on the tap and warm water cascaded down on us. I took the bar of soap from the metal holder and held it out to her.

"Let me watch how you soap yourself."

For a couple of seconds she hesitated. Then she took the bar and ran it across her chest, under her arms, and around her neck. Soap suds slid down her beautiful body. Fuck, I couldn't wait to get inside her. Then, with adorable shyness, she swiped it between her legs.

"Don't stop," I growled.

She raised her arms and bent her elbows to do her back. Her breasts jutted forward. I wanted to suck the pink tips into my mouth. Sheepishly, she did the crack of her ass. I watched her do her thighs and legs. She picked up her foot to clean the sole of her foot. The action revealed the delicate, pink folds of her pussy. I stared, transfixed. She put the foot down and raised the other. Showing me another eyeful. Water beat down on my cock, making it bounce. It was so fucking hard it was fucking tingling.

I bent down and took her nipplesbetween my teeth. Water ran into my mouth, changing the normal sensation of having a woman's nipple in my mouth. In my life time I'd been in the shower with hundreds of women. I'd taken all their nipples in my mouth, but when I took hers I didn't feel like it was a simple exchange of pleasure: I make you see stars, you make me come.

No, with her, I felt like eating her alive, consuming her. I wanted to go on my knees and fucking feast on her pussy for days. I couldn't imagine letting anyone else have her. I wanted to keep her forever. I felt like she was *mine*.

I sucked hard enough to cause her pain, because she gasped.

I lifted my head. "Do you want me to stop?"

"No," she whispered her eyes wide and dilated. Her eyelashes were full of water.

I took her other nipple in my mouth and sucked it gently, and she moaned sensuously. The sound sent me wild.

I turned her around so she was facing the tiled wall. Very firmly, I grabbed her hips and tilted them upwards. Then I got on my haunches. I grabbed the flesh of her cheeks and pulling them apart blew on her glistening sex. She shivered with anticipation. I buried my face between her cheeks and… I feasted. This time I couldn't stop. I sucked, I licked, and I bit the plump flesh. Even her whimpers didn't stop me. I ravished her like I had never ravished another. I sucked until she shuddered and climaxed sobbing.

My cock was hot and hungry so I felt the blood surging urgently through it. If I didn't get into her soon, I was going to fucking explode.

I pulled her out of the shower and positioned her in front of the sink.

"I want you to watch me fuck you in the mirror. Hands on the sink, legs spread, ass sticking out," I told her. While she stood gripping the sink hard, legs apart, and pushing her curvy ass as high as it would go, I retrieved the condom I left on the counter.

"Play with your clit," I ordered.

Her back arched even more as she obeyed. It made her ass go higher, and her whole sweet pussy hung between her legs and begged me to fuck it. My favorite pose for a woman.

Perfect. Just fucking perfect.

I grabbed her hips and slid into her. I rammed so far into her body, her eyes widened in the mirror. I fucked her hard from the back while I watched her hand as it circled her clit. It was so engorged with blood it protruded out. We carried on like that, our wet bodies slapping, our eyes locked on each other in the mirror. I fucked her so hard the Field's designer sink began to creak. Finally, with an animal-like cry, that I muffled with my hand, she came hard on my dick. She always went over the edge so beautifully.

There was no holding back after that.

I exploded deep inside her. I didn't immediately slide out of her. We stood there joined and breathing hard, as I stroked her hair. Pushing it away from the back of her neck, I kissed the smooth wet flesh.

I looked up and her eyes were sparkling, her cheeks were flushed, her swollen mouth slightly open and panting. I had never seen a woman look more achingly beautiful.

She belonged to me now. Every fucking inch of her was mine.

*J*t was nearly eight o'clock. After a toe-curling shower, I'd sat in the easy chair with my e-reader and finished one book, then started another.

Serenity. That was the word for it. A beautiful, serene world full of beautiful people.

From my window, I could make out the back of the property and the lake just beyond it. Max was out there, somewhere, and a few other boats dotted the water. The sky was deep blue, clear, and it seemed like I could see for miles. And it was all lovely. I wished I could take a picture that would accurately capture it all, but no camera could do that.

It was enough to sit and breathe it in, to know I was part of it for a little while before going back to the noise and congestion of the city. I loved it, of course, but I was starting to see the value of being able to get away sometimes.

A couple of hours later, when the thought of coffee was too much to resist, I contemplated going downstairs. After dressing in jeans, a fitted button-down, and cardigan—I'd done my fair share of research before packing, and that seemed to be a popular clothing combination—I went down to the kitchen. There, Millicent and Gretchen sat with their coffee. Fortunately, there was no sign of Lillian.

"Mimi, sweetheart, help yourself. Cora has the morning off, so we're sort of pitching in to do things on our own. I hope you don't mind."

"Not at all," I said.

Pouring a cup of coffee was hardly a hardship. And of course, it was the best coffee I'd ever tasted, because why wouldn't it be? Everything was perfect there.

The kitchen was stunning, a chef's dream come true. Stainless steel appliances, a six-burner gas range, dual ovens, even a wood-fired oven built into the wall. I couldn't imagine what they baked in there. Pizza? Bread? Either way, I'd happily taste test.

The ladies sat in what I guessed was the breakfast nook, a sunny spot in the back corner of the room which faced out in the direction my room did. Millicent waved me over. I wondered what Gretchen thought of that. How much did she know about me? If Lillian had told her, she hid it well. Either that or she thought her soon-to-be son-in-law was as big a piece of garbage as he actually was.

"The boys should be back soon from their little trip," Millicent chuckled.

Gretchen's nose wrinkled in distaste. "I simply can't understand the allure of fishing."

"I reacted the same way when Max told me he was going," I confided. "I'm not much of an outdoorsy girl, I guess. Though I do like hiking."

"Sure. It doesn't involve slimy fish and worms." The three of us grinned, and I thought I didn't hate Gretchen as much as I'd assumed I would.

Until she opened her mouth again. "So exactly how long have you and Max been together? I heard you were already in another relationship until just recently."

My blood turned to ice. Millicent, bless her heart, looked confused. Whether or not she actually was, I had no idea. I felt like a deer about to be run over by a semi with sweet, pretty Gretchen at the wheel. There I was, worrying about people taking Max and me for a fake when I should've been coming up with a rebuttal for a question about Josh. Finally, I managed to squeak out, "I wouldn't call it a relationship. It was all under false pretenses."

"Oh, was it?" She leaned her chin on her hand, all innocence.

"Yes, and I was deeply hurt when I found out the truth." I stared at her, almost daring her to keep going. I didn't want to embarrass Millicent by flinging my dirty laundry around, but I'd go there if Gretchen kept pushing.

She didn't. Instead of running me down, she sat back in her chair. "Well, I'm sorry to hear that."

"So was I."

"How about some cake?" Millicent asked, smiling almost too brightly.

"None for me, thanks. I think I'll take a little walk."

I went out without my coat and was glad to find it unseasonably warm outside. I wouldn't have to suffer the cold while I sulked. I couldn't stay in there a minute longer, not with Judgy McJudgepants staring at me over the rim of her coffee cup. I should've known she would find some thinly-veiled way of bringing Josh into the conversation. Well, I wasn't ill-bred enough to tell the whole sordid story, though that would've been just what Josh deserved.

I would never do it anyway. Lillian made my skin crawl and I wouldn't have minded if she moved to Nepal and never came back, but it wasn't her fault her boyfriend cheated. She was just a woman, like me.

I guessed I would've freaked out the way she did if the shoe was on the other foot, but I would have dropped Josh like a freaking scalding-hot potato if I'd found out what she did. Good luck to her. She wanted to stand by her man, even when he wasn't much of a man.

There was a wooded area beyond the painstakingly mani-cured lawn, and I walked toward it. Maybe a little time around nature would make me feel less homicidal. Max was bound to come back soon, and nobody would be mean to me when he was around. They wouldn't dare. He was one of them.

When I saw a figure emerging from the trees, my heart skipped a beat. It was Max coming to look for me. Too cold for outdoor sex, but it would be nice to walk with him.

But it wasn't.

I looked up at the sky and laughed when I realized it was Josh walking toward me. *Was this my punishment for being so happy? What next? A phone call to tell me my apartment had burned to the ground?*

"What are you laughing about?" he asked as he approached.

We were out of sight of the house, which was at least a relief. I didn't need anybody spying on us, thinking we were sneaking around together. Like I would sneak around with Josh if he paid me in gold bars and designer shoes.

"Nothing worth talking about," I replied with a slight frown. I did not want to encourage him to hang around me out here.

He glanced back in the direction of the house, probably wondering as I had whether we were out of sight. "There's something I've been meaning to talk to you about," he said, his eyes shifting toward the house every so often as he spoke. Right then, he looked what he was. A slimy creep.

"There's nothing I want to talk with you about, Josh. We've already said all there is to say."

I tried to walk around him, but he stepped in front of me. I went the other way, and he blocked me again. Finally, gathering my courage, I stepped up and laying both my hands on his chest, pushed him away as hard as I could. Instead of backing off, he grabbed me by the arms.

"What the hell are you doing?" I asked furiously. I tried to wrestle my way out of his grasp, but he was too strong.

"Would you stop fighting me, damn it? I'm not trying to hurt you. I just wanted to tell you I was wrong. I made a big mistake."

"Oh, get off it, Josh. Let me go."

"Not until you listen to what I have to say."

"Say it, fast, then never touch me again." I glared at him, ready to spit in his face.

"You don't mean that."

"Oh, try me. I wish you would."

His face fell. "I know you're angry with me. You can't be angrier with me than I am."

I sighed with exasperation. "Get to the point please."

"Don't you get what I'm trying to tell you? I made the biggest mistake of my life when I let you go. I want you back."

I was so stunned, I stopped pulling away. My mouth fell open. Just when I thought I'd heard it all he comes up with *this*. Where does this man get off?

"Were you dropped on your head when you were a baby?" I gasped when I got my voice and the ability to use it back.

"What?" His eyes searched my face desperately. "Mimi, I know you're pissed with me, but you can't pretend you don't feel what's still there between us."

"I'm not pretending," I said through clenched teeth. "There is no 'us', Josh. There never was. You were never honest with me, and if I didn't have to work with you, I'd happily never see your cheating face again." I yanked my arms away from him, pushing him again for good measure. "And don't ever lay your hands on me again. Ever."

"I love you, Mimi."

I just about told him to go straight to hell when a tall, dark blur broke into my line of vision and shoved Josh away much more forcefully than I ever could have. I gasped when I saw Max standing in front of me, hands curled into fists.

"What do you think you're doing?" he asked in a low, deadly tone. I was actually afraid for Josh just then.

"This isn't any of your business. She was my girlfriend first," Josh spat when he got his balance back.

Max's right fist cocked back just a split second before it pistoned out, catching Josh's mouth. He fell to the ground, hand flying up to the lip Max had just split.

"Are you insane?" Josh asked, his words muffled.

Max took a step toward him, making him scramble backward like a terrified little animal. "No. You are if you ever touch her again," Max replied in that same deadly tone of voice. He pointed up toward the house. "You're so damn lucky we're here and not out on the street somewhere—it would be in your best interest to not cross my path again after this weekend. And if you're smart, you'll go back indoors and tell them you tripped in the woods and hit your lip on some rocks. Unless you want your in-laws and your boss to find out about you manhandling Mimi and trying to dump your pregnant fiancée. I used to think you weren't good enough for Mimi. Now I know you're not even good enough for Lillian."

If there was ever a time I wanted to jump the man and promise to have his babies while ripping his clothes off, that was it. He took my hand without saying a word and led me back to the house. I heard him breathing hard and fast through his flared nostrils, like an animal on the verge of attack.

"Thank you for that," I breathed.

"He won't do it again," he muttered. "He fucking better not, or I'll break his damn jaw."

"I think he got the message loud and clear," I said softly.

"Is your hand okay?" He looked at me with the expression of a man who couldn't believe he'd heard what he just did, so I guess that meant he was all right.

It was the like the weekend of things I'd never done. Visiting the Hamptons. Sex in the shower. And now, two men had fought over me. One had even punched the other. Megan would shit a brick when I told her.

53

MIMI

When we got back to the house the first person we met was Lillian. She looked at me suspiciously.

"Have you seen Josh?"

"Nope," I lied without batting an eyelid.

"I wonder where he is," she said, still staring at me.

"He might be out taking a walk. The woods are nice this time of the year," Max said.

"It's too cold to go out walking. I'm not supposed to exert myself. I'll wait for him in the conservatory."

Max nodded. "Mimi and I are going upstairs for a...nap."

I flushed to the roots of my hair and Lillian's head snapped around to me. I stared at her in astonishment. Oh, my God, she was jealous of me. She wanted my man!

Max tugged my hand and we walked up the grand staircase.

He pulled me into the room, kicked the door shut and started to undress me.

"Whoa," I said, surprised.

"I hated seeing him put his hands on you. You belong to me," he said, his eyes blazing with need.

His face looked cruel and beautiful as he crashed his lips on mine. Burning heat flowered in my core. All thought ceases to exist. With his mouth fused with mine, he was tearing away my clothes. Until I was standing in front of him naked.

"I'm going in raw this time," he said, unbuttoning his jeans and pushing them down his slim hips roughly. His cock was so hard it was sticking out over the waistband of his underwear.

I looked down as it nodded. I wanted him too. He would be the first man I ever allowed such a thing, but an electric current of pure excitement raced up my spine. There was something completely primal about a man filling you with his seed. It was like an ancient pact; a man who took a woman and marked her with his semen. He turned me around and grabbing my hips with both hands he thrust so deeply into me, I cried out.

Like a greedy hussy, I pushed back and ground myself into him.

He grabbed a fistful of my hair and pulled my head back. While he fucked me ruthlessly, he growled, "you're fucking mine."

I gasped with pleasure.

"Say it," he commanded.

"I'm yours," I cried.

He sucked the side of my neck hard. I knew what he was doing. Like a wild animal, he was leaving his mark. He was telling everyone I was his. I stretched my neck and offered it to him, to lick, to suck, to bite.

"Play with yourself," he ordered close to my ear.

I obeyed immediately, my fingers working furiously, as he pounded me from behind. His cock rammed into me, and his balls slapped against me as my climax began. My knees locked and body began to convulse and clench uncontrollably. I thought I would fall.

"I'm coming," I cried.

He tightened his hold on me and slammed so brutally into me, pain mixed with the pleasure. A loud deep groan rumbled in his chest as he emptied his warm cum into my pussy. The aftershocks of my climax made my thighs tremble. He thrust slowly in and out of me. His grip on my hair loosened. His hand brushed strands of hair away from my face and neck. Then he gently kissed my neck while his hand traveled down to splay over my stomach and tightly hug my body.

"I loved that," I whispered, my heart pulsing.

"You're the only woman who has ever made my cock ache for her."

The air left my lungs in a long sigh of contentment. I don't know how long we remained in that position, with him just cradling me, until a sound from the outside world intruded.

"I've cleaned all the downstairs bathrooms. I'll be starting with the Green Room next," someone called in the corridor outside.

I turned to look into Max's eyes. He smiled softly.

"Of course, Max won't be winning any angling competitions any time soon," Alexander teased during dinner.

Max shrugged good-naturedly, much calmer than he was when we first got back to the house earlier that morning. "I can't be good at everything."

I caught Josh hurling a nasty look his way, but only I saw it. Everybody else was busy laughing.

"How's your lip, Josh?" Gretchen looked concerned—and maybe slightly amused? I couldn't tell. Even if she somehow blamed me for seducing her daughter's fella, she had to hold him responsible, too. Maybe she enjoyed seeing him hurt a little. A total mama bear.

He shrugged, looking down at his bowl of soup. He couldn't handle much more than that, or so he said, since opening his mouth too wide hurt too much. "It'll be fine," he mumbled.

Alexander nodded sagely, his bald dome gleaming in the light from the overhead chandelier. "Gotta be careful in those woods, my boy. You never know what you'll run into."

Max snorted quietly, his head down. I kicked him under the table. He kicked me back, though not as hard. We'd finally been able to laugh about it after a little while. Josh hadn't hurt me, and it would be a very cold day in Hell before I ever considered being with him again.

Life was good, I thought with a satisfied smile. I had a man in my life who was willing to fight for me. No matter what happened when we got home, there was no way we could go back to being just friends. I had seen his 'O' face. You can't go back from that no matter how hard you try.

And I was sitting in a gorgeous dining room in a home I would never have had the chance to visit otherwise. With genuinely nice people, for the most part. Max found my hand, resting on my lap, and squeezed. I squeezed back, wondering what that night would bring. We were both wearing entirely too much clothing, as far as I was concerned. From the way he released my hand and started stroking my thigh, I could tell he felt the same way.

"So, Max." Alexander's strident voice broke into our little moment. "How are things going at work?"

"Oh, just fine." I was intrigued. Max never talked about work. I might finally get to hear about it.

"And how's that pesky little troll you've been dealing with?"

To my surprise, Max pales. He becomes white under his tan.

"You know," Alexander says with a mocking laugh, "the one who won't leave her apartment?"

*M*ax's hand froze. So did my entire body. Including my heart.

"What's this all about?" Peter asked, looking in our direction.

Alexander jumped in when Max didn't say anything right away. "He's been trying for months to get one last tenant out of her apartment so he can finally go ahead with renovating the entire building into luxury apartments. But she won't budge, the pain in the…well, you know. It's been a bit of a setback. There's always gotta be one holdout, doesn't there?"

I looked down at my plate, fighting back the tears that threatened to spill over. Max's hand was still on my thigh, so I picked it up by the wrist and dropped it on his own leg. The entire world was crashing in on me and the rest of the table talked and joked as though nothing was happening. How was that possible? How? I was dying inside. I couldn't sit there for another moment.

"What are you going to do with this woman?" Gretchen asked curiously.

"I suggested he seduce her," Alexander said with a laugh.

"Excuse me," I whispered, pushing my chair back.

"Oh, that was before I knew he was going out with you, obviously," Alexander blurted out, suddenly realizing what he had said.

I took pains to look casual, I even managed to smile sweetly at everyone on the table. "Don't worry. It's nothing you said. I'm just not feeling very well. I think I'll go upstairs and lie down for a bit. Enjoy your dinner."

I could see Millicent wanted to ask me what was wrong, but I walked out of the room before her question could be asked.

I heard Max mumbling something about checking on me, so I knew he was following. As soon as I was away from the dining room, I dashed to the stairs and ran all the way up. By the time Max reached the bedroom, I was already packing.

"Hang on. Let me explain," he whispered urgently.

"Don't say a word, Max. If you don't want me to cause a scene and embarrass us both, you'll go back downstairs to dinner and forget you ever knew me."

"What are you doing? Are you leaving?" He stood beside the dresser as I grabbed blindly at my things, shoving them into the suitcase. "Please, Mimi. Listen to me. You have to give me a chance."

"I don't have to give you shit," I whispered.

"Just listen to me."

"Are you the developer?" I asked.

"Yes," he confessed.

I shook my head. "How could you? How could you!"

He reached out a hand to grab my hand and I recoiled as if he was a striking snake. "I swear, I'm going to scream this house down if you don't leave me alone, Max. You need to get out of this room. Now."

"How will you get out of here?" he asked.

"I'll get an Uber. No big deal."

"Uber? All the way back to the city?"

"What the hell do you care?" I turned away, pushing my clothes and toiletries down so I could close the zipper. "Don't start pretending to care about me now, Max. It's pretty low."

"I do care. You know I care." I heard the urgency in his voice, the desperation even. And part of me wanted to give in and give him a chance to explain himself, but what could he say to make things better. He was the developer and he had taken Alexander's advice and seduced me. The only problem was, I was not going anywhere. He was going to have to build his precious apartments around me. I thought he was one of the good guys. I let myself fall in love with him.

I wished I were dead.

I wished he were dead.

I looked up from my bag to find him pale-faced, worry lines creased his forehead. For once, he didn't look sophisticated. All it took was a slip of somebody else's tongue to turn him from a god into a despicable human being.

"I don't know anything about you," I spat. "And you kept it that way. Never talking about work, about where your money comes from, or what you do with it. Oh, unless you were trying to impress me with your limo and your concert tickets and your fucking friends in the fucking Hamptons. Now I understand why."

"Mimi, please…"

"Oh, you don't want them to hear me?" I sneered. "Don't worry about it. Nobody needs to know that the great Max Black would stoop low enough to seduce a woman just to get her apartment. Ugh. Sickening"

"Oh, my God. That's what you think? Mimi, that's crazy." He took a step toward me.

"Don't come any closer," I warned. "I mean it. Don't even think about touching me, either. It's over. Whatever this is, whatever we had, it's done. And for the record, you'll never get that apartment from me, so bad luck. I hope I never lay eyes on you again. I thought Josh was bad, but he's got nothing on you." I raised one arm, pointing to the door. "Now get out before I start screaming. I mean it. Everybody's going to know what you did if you don't leave right now."

He raised both his hands and backed away, looking stricken. "All right. What do you want me to tell everybody?" he asked.

"Don't you get it? I don't give a fuck what you say to them. They're not my friends. Tell them I'm sick. Tell them I found out I hate you. Whatever. You decide. You're good at making things up."

I pulled out my phone with shaking hands and opened the Uber app to request a car. When I looked up again, he was gone.

I collapsed onto the bed, shaking from head to toe, but I couldn't cry. Not yet. Not until I was far away. I couldn't run the risk of him seeing me fall apart.

✳

*I*n a daze, I looked up at the steel-gray sky with its fast-moving clouds. We would get early snow out of those clouds. It smelled like snow, the air holding that certain special scent it only got before a storm.

The first available cab would be here in an hour's time. I was already waiting outside for it. It was a hell of a tab, but it was a small price for getting out of there as quickly as possible.

Max had tried to wait with me. Maybe he wanted to talk or explain and make new excuses, but I turned on him with such venom, he raised both his hands in a gesture of appeasement and went back inside.

When the car pulled up to the house, I went down the steps, pulling my suitcase behind me, my laptop and purse over one shoulder. I felt bruised, beaten, ready to give up. There had been only one place I could imagine going just then. Ever since Grandma died and Mom and I drifted apart, but I had always felt sad about it. Right now. I needed her.

"Wow, nice place?" the driver said.

"Yeah," I said quietly and stared out of the window. He probably thought I was a snob. He didn't know my heart was broken. Half-way through the journey, I started sobbing my heart out. The poor driver must have thought I was insane.

55

MIMI

om was waiting at the door for me. She held it open as I maneuvered myself and my bags inside. I hadn't told her why I was coming, only that I was on my way and needed her very badly. She took one look at my swollen, tear-stained face and opened her arms for me to step into her embrace.

"What happened, baby? Who hurt you?"

"Oh, Mom. I can't believe it. I'm such an idiot."

"I'm sure it's not your fault," she murmured, stroking my hair as I shook with fresh sobs.

"I've been so stupid."

"Come on. I'll fix us some tea and we'll talk it out. I'm sure it'll be all right. Everything looks better after a pot of tea."

One of my grandmother's favorite sayings passed down to my Mom and then to me. The thought of her, of that apartment I loved so much, only made me feel worse. My chest hurt, literal physical pain. I wondered if I was having a heart attack. Maybe that was what happened when a person's heart broke. They had a heart attack and died and didn't have to hurt anymore.

I finished crying in the time it took the water to boil and splashed my face as the tea steeped. Mom waited until I was seated in one of the little wooden chairs around her small kitchen table before asking any questions.

"What happened, sweetie?"

I poured the whole thing out. Josh, Max, the way he'd saved me when I was cornered. The way we pretended to be a couple. She smiled when I told her about hurting my ankle, and the way he'd been so sweet to me. I even hinted at things moving to the next level with Max without getting graphic. We were friends and all, me and my mom, but we weren't that close.

And then I told her about what Alexander said at dinner. She knew about the buyer who tried to get me to move out, of course, and she covered her mouth with her hands. "Oh, no. Oh, that's horrible!" She looked genuinely heartbroken, just like any mother would when their child was in pain.

"So, that's what happened. I came here instead of going all the way home. I couldn't imagine being there alone right now."

"Of course, honey. I'm so glad you came. I'm so sorry this happened." She patted my hand, wiping away her own tears with the other.

"Is it me? Am I a magnet for these jerks who think they can use women and get away with it?"

She shook her head. "Of course, you're not. You're just having a run of bad luck."

"That's putting it mildly," I whispered. The tea did help a little, at least. Chamomile. Just the scent relaxed me, and the memory of nights spent drinking tea together tugged at my bruised heart.

"I thought I was in love with him, Mom. I'm so ashamed of myself."

She clucked her tongue in sympathy. "That's nothing to be ashamed of. You can't blame yourself for developing feelings for him. He sounds like the total package when you don't include the apartment issue."

"That was what I thought, too. I thought he had it all. And he wanted me, which obviously made him even more attractive."

We both snorted into our teacups, which ended in a sob for me.

"Let me pass on a little bit of wisdom I've picked up," she said, her voice as soft and gentle as ever.

"Please, do. I'm in dire need."

"There's nothing to be ashamed of. Love isn't something that's supposed to make us feel ashamed."

"But I let myself fall for him, Mom. It's embarrassing."

"I know it is right now, but you still have nothing to be ashamed of. Just because it didn't work out doesn't mean your feelings weren't real. I mean, look at your father and me." She grinned ruefully, shaking her head. "Ahh, I know it's hard for you to believe this, but there was a time when we were crazy about each other. When we didn't fight constantly. We were really, truly in love. And just because it ended the way it did, doesn't erase those feelings. That would be a terrible shame, wouldn't it?"

"It would."

"You might wish you never felt that way," she said, nodding. "I used to. I used to wish I never met him. But then I wouldn't have you. And I wouldn't have the memory of when times were good. I can't pretend I would erase the memory if I had the chance. Just like I'm sure you wouldn't erase the memory of Max if you had a chance to do it."

I wanted to disagree with her, but it was no use. She was always right, as I'd come to understand the older I got. Wouldn't thirteen-year-old me be disappointed? "You're right. I wouldn't."

"You know you can stay as long as you need, right?"

"Can I just stay forever?"

She shook her head. "Afraid not. You can't hide from life forever."

"Ugh. You sound so much like a mom right now."

"It's an occupational hazard."

"Mom, something has always bothered me."

"What"

"Why do you think Grandma left the apartment to me and not you?"

She shrugged. "You sure you want to know?"

I frowned. What new surprises would I have to deal with today? "Of course."

"Your grandma had a gift. She never spoke about it, but when we were kids she used to sometimes use it."

"What gift?" I whispered.

"She knew things. She would say, Oh, Uncle Ermine must be sick and then we would get news that Uncle Ermine was indeed sick. Sometimes she'd say, oh, I think Fleur might come to visit today and sure enough Fleur would come. Mind you these were the days before the internet. Three days before her father passed away she knew and she began picking wild flowers for his funeral. She was only five years old then."

"Wow. Really?" I breathed.

Mom nodded. "The reason she wanted you to have the apartment was that she said the most important thing that would ever happen to you would happen when you were living there. She almost wrote it into her will that you couldn't sell it during your lifetime."

I stared at mom in astonishment.

Mom patted my hand gently. "She didn't want me to tell you because she didn't want you to change your behavior in any way, but she was very old at that time and I don't know if her gift was still strong. She could have been wrong."

I looked at my mother bitterly. "I guess she was wrong. The apartment has brought me my greatest hurt and betrayal. I don't know if I can ever trust another man again, Mom."

"Oh, darling. If you want to sell that apartment and move on you can. I know, if she could see you now, she wouldn't expect you to live there. She just wanted what was best for you."

❄

*T*here was nothing like being home with Mom when my heart hurt. Running home to be with Mommy should be a requirement for all people trying to act like grownups. Sometimes, being a grown up hurt too much. When I went up to my old room I almost wished my Barbie Dream House were still there so I could really regress.

She even made me instant mac and cheese for lunch on Sunday because she knew me that well and was pretty much the best mother on the planet. We watched old movies like we used to when I was a kid and things at home were good. I couldn't help remembering when I teased Max about watching them. It would be a while before every little thing didn't remind me of him.

I told myself to stop watching the clock since all that did was remind me that every passing minute put me one minute closer to needing to go home. The thought of running into Max nauseated me. I didn't know what he'd want from me, and I sure didn't know how I'd keep living there with the knowledge that he was on the other side of the floor. I couldn't exactly get away with egging his door or leaving burning dog poop in the hall. He'd sort of know it was me. And I'd have to smell the burning poop, too, so that was another mark in the negative column.

He didn't even try to call. That was the worst part. He knew my number. He'd texted me in the past. He didn't try to text after I left. Was he really that willing to let go of me? Even Josh had tried to reach out, for God's sake.

The light outside dimmed, and I looked out the window to see clouds rolling in. It was only fitting, considering my mood. I could go for a good storm just then.

"I'm going to get dinner started," Mom announced.

"What's for dinner?"

"What do you think?"

"Spaghetti and meatballs?"

She nodded with a smile. "I know my girl."

"I'm going to ask again. Can I just stay here forever?"

"And again I have to say no," she replied. "This is special occasion-level stuff. Any other night and we'd have sandwiches and soup."

"Blargh." I stuck my tongue out at her. She was still chuckling as she walked into the kitchen from the neat, cheerful little living room. I'd lived there with her after the divorce, which made it tough to spend time in the city. I loved going to my grandmother's home when my parent were fighting, but Mom's house would always mean love to me. Hence my running there when somebody hurt me.

The difference between it and the Fields Estate was staggering, but I'd rather be in a little two-bedroom on Long Island. Especially when nobody there had lied to me.

I thought I might have heard the cushions sigh in relief as my butt left the couch for the first time all day to return to my apartment.

56

MIMI

I was sitting on my couch pouring my shattered heart out to Megan when the doorbell rang.

"You expecting anybody?" Megan asked as I got off the couch.

"No," I said. I lived in an apartment building. There was no such thing as random people at the door. I put my eye to the spy hole in the door and flew backward in shock.

"Who is it? Is it him?" Megan asked.

"Yes," I whispered.

"You have knives in the kitchen, right?"

"That's very helpful, Megan."

The bell went again and I jumped.

"Aren't you going to answer it?"

I debated on opening the door, honestly. Should I? Or should I leave him swinging in the wind? And why was he there?

"Yeah, I'll call you back," I said and flung the door open before I could talk myself out of it. And there he was, standing there looking absolutely gorgeous.

"What do you want?" I barked as I folded my arms, and glared at him. Really, I was only trying to protect myself. I closed myself off physically to remind myself to close off emotionally. I couldn't let him in, even though my heart wanted to reach out to him. He looked so damn handsome. How was that even remotely fair? Meanwhile, I was wearing the same leggings and sweatshirt I'd slept in and my hair hadn't been brushed all day, just thrown up in a bun.

I saw red. I mean I didn't even think I just reacted. It was like a wall of fury just slammed into my brain. My hand shot out and I slapped him so hard my hand hurt. For a second he went absolutely still then he moved.

So fast, I didn't have time to move.

He picked me up, threw me unceremoniously over his shoulder, and carried me to my bedroom kicking, screaming, and punching his back with my clenched fists. I might as well not have bothered for all the attention he paid me. He kicked open my bedroom door and it slammed hard against the wall. He threw me on the bed and looked down at me.

I looked up at him breathing hard, hating him. "Get out of my apartment, you shitty bastard," I yelled.

Suddenly he fell on me pinning me down. I opened my mouth to scream and he silenced me with the palm of his hand. I tried to bite his palm but could find no purchase.

He stared into my eyes.

I struggled hard until there was no energy left in any of my limbs and I went slack. Tears of frustration welled up in my eyes and streamed down the sides of my face. He raised his palm and I opened my mouth to scream again.

This time he covered my mouth with his own.

It was a kiss like nothing he had ever given me before. It was full of aggression, and anger, and passion. The more I tried to stay unaffected the harder he kissed me. He forced his tongue past my lips and swept it into my mouth looking for mine. He hooked my tongue, took into his own mouth and sucked it hard. Eventually, I became lost in his kiss and my hands curled around his neck.

He lifted his head. "I didn't mean to lie to you."

"You still did."

He caught my hands and pinned them over my head.

"Let go of me, you monster," I said struggling against the band of steel around my wrists.

Holding my wrists above my head, he grabbed my shirt and tore it open.

"Fuck you," I said fiercely, but I didn't want him to stop. My stomach leaped with excitement.

"I plan to," he growled thickly and ripped the lace on my bra making my breast pop out. He bit the tip. I swore, then moaned with intense pleasure as he began to suck it.

His hand slid between my legs. My body was screaming for him. I heard my panties tear, and then with his eyes never leaving me, he unbuckled his pants, a feral look in his eyes.

A moan of anticipation left my lips. He spread my thighs with his knee, and entered me with such force I shot up on the bed and screamed. It was as though we were fucking for the first time. My pussy was so tight and clenched, even he looked surprised. "This is the last fucking time you run away from me," he said and pulling out of me thrust in again.

"Did you hear me?" Thrust.

"Fuck you," I spat.

"You're mine and you don't run away no matter what." Thrust.

"Oh God...you, you lied to me."

"You don't know that. You didn't hear my side of the story." Thrust.

I opened my mouth to speak and he put his palm over my mouth "Don't say another word until you've heard my side. Do you understand?"

I nodded silently. He took his palm off my mouth and I lost myself to one of the most amazing sex sessions of my life. It was just primal lust. We were both wild and ruthless. He gave no quarter; I asked for none. He bit me, I scratched his back. It was just hard thrusts and the kind of climax where it felt like an explosion in my soul. I clung to his shoulders and screamed my head off. And he let me. Why not? We had the whole building to ourselves.

His cock was still semi-hard and inside me when I turned my head to the side. I hated that I lost control. That I let him into my body when he had betrayed me.

"Now get off me," I panted harshly.

"*N*o. Not until I've said what I wanted to say."

"You've already said everything I need to know in WASP heaven."

"No, if you remember, I didn't get to say anything. You packed and left."

"Oh, right. I bet I'm supposed to think this is cute, huh? The man who'll stop at nothing to get to me. You don't see how shitty it looks from my side. Invading my privacy just so you can get the last word, far away from your cronies." I rolled my eyes. "Sorry if I don't swoon."

"Really, Mimi? That is what you think this is all about? Me getting the last word."

"Isn't it?"

"I don't give a shit what they or anybody else thinks about me. I do what I want to do. Alex is your boss not mine. I let you go because I didn't want to spoil it for *you*. I knew you were determined to make a scene and I didn't want to give them anything to gossip about. Eventually, those people are going to be your friends too. Besides, I wanted this to end with a screaming orgasm worth of an empty building."

I turned my head away, feeling confused. His words were making me think he wanted to be with me, and when I looked at him, it was too hard to stay level-headed. "Okay, so you're here. What do you have to say?"

He touched my cheek gently and I closed my eyes so that he couldn't see how much I wanted that.

"There's so much."

"Start at the beginning and hurry up about it," I said between gritted teeth. I was fast losing control of the situation.

"Okay, fine. I wanted to tell you about the development that first night."

"Bullshit," I spat.

"See? I can't talk to you if you're gonna shut me down like that." His voice was firm.

"Fine. I won't interrupt."

"I wanted to tell you. I thought it would only be right. I felt like an ass. Like I was lying by omission."

"Because you were."

"Because I was," he agreed. "But you were so drunk, and then you started crying. I wasn't gonna be like, hey, by the way, I'm actually the guy who wants you out of your apartment. If you were me, would you have said it then?"

"No."

"Exactly because contrary to what you think I'm not that much of a dick."

I looked at him out of the corner of my eye.

"I don't know, Mimi. You did something to me that night."

"What did I do to you? Please, don't lie to me right now. I can't take it."

"I'm telling you the truth. Before I met you, I mean really met you that night, I thought you were a gorgeous pain in the ass. You were holding me back from going ahead with my plans. I had no time for your stupid stubbornness. You were rejecting offers that were well above market price, but when I met you. I started to respect you. Most of the people I know are so rich all they have is money. You had everything. You were funny and smart, and kind, and sexy and beautiful. I liked you from that night on. You were a real person."

"Jeez, I was finally a real person. I wish I had known. I would've bought a card to congratulate myself," I babbled because I didn't know how else to respond.

"So that's what happened."

"I feel like we're skipping a really important part of this story."

"What?"

I finally turned my head to look at him. "The part where you never told me the truth after that. You had so many chances to come clean, Max. Why didn't you ever tell me the truth?"

"Honestly?"

"Jesus, Max."

"Because I wanted you to like me, too. I wanted you to get to

265

know me as a person and not some nameless villain. Hell, especially when I knew how much the apartment meant to you. I figured if you got to know me and liked me..."

"You could seduce me out of my apartment."

"No. You would understand why I was working on getting you out of there in the first place. You would, I don't know, forgive me or something. But the more time that passed, the worse it got."

"My heart breaks for you right now."

"I'm serious."

"Me too."

He shook his head. "All right. I'm a dick. Does that make you feel better? I said it. I'm a dick."

"Yes, Max. That makes me feel so much better. Wow. Thank you. You can go now."

I was still furious and more embarrassed than ever. "You were just using me, no matter how you try to spin it. Trying to get me to like you. It was all a big lie. You played up what was happening between us so I'd like you more. You were being fake all the time, is that it? Just faking me out just to get my apartment."

"No! You don't understand anything. I don't want your apartment. I've already had designs drawn up around your apartment."

"Good for you," I said sarcastically.

"You still don't get it. I don't care about any of that. I'm in love with you, Mimi Young."

I stared at him in shock. "What did you say?"

He grinned. "I said, I'm in love with you."

"Oh." My heart pounded a mile a minute. I swallowed hard. "I wasn't expecting that."

"Sorry. I didn't mean to freak you out."

I looked him in the eye, searching for the truth. He looked sincere. He sounded sincere, too. His face was full of what looked like hope and anticipation combined.

"Do you mean it?" I asked. "I mean, really? You're not just saying that so I'll give you a blowjob?"

His eyes popped open. "Will you?"

"I don't know. I don't know. I might."

He placed one hand over mine, right over my heart. "I mean it. I started to fall for you from that first night. I told myself it was just lust, but it wasn't, and I've been working my ass off since then to get you to feel the same way." He shrugged. "It's lame. I know it is. But that's what happened."

I took a deep breath, cold air filling my lungs. "Wow. But I was so drunk."

"You were mega drunk," he smirked. "And mega cute and sexy and a phenomenal kisser. That helped, too. I'm crazy about you."

I smiled, still sure I was dreaming. But no, it was too vivid for a dream. I could feel the weight of his hard body, and the scent of his cologne mixed with our coupling. His hand was warm, and my heart raced so hard I could have sworn my chest would burst.

"I love you," I whispered, terrified and elated and relieved to finally let it out.

His face lit up, a smile spreading from ear to ear. "You do?"

"Why do you think I was so upset last night? That wasn't because of an apartment, or because you lied. It was because I'm totally, stupidly in love with you."

Anything I was about to say was cut off by his kiss. I threw my arms around him and kissed him back.

He loved me. He loved me!

I touched my forehead to his, breathing deep, wanting to take that moment and hold it in my heart forever.

"What do you say we find a way to be together forever?" he asked.

"I think I could get on board with that."

"As long as you don't ask me to start drinking coconut water."

"As long as you don't ask me to start running."

"I love you."

"I love you." I couldn't have wiped the smile off my face if I tried. Then, something occurred to me. "Do you like spaghetti and meatballs?"

"Who doesn't?"

"Think you might wanna meet my mom?"

He grinned. "Mothers love me."

"Mine's pretty tough."

"Like mother, like daughter, then."

"You sure you're up to the challenge?" And I didn't mean just meeting my mother. I meant being together, meshing our lives, creating one of our own. I could see myself with him forever, scary as the word felt. When I looked into his eyes, it didn't feel all that scary, after all. Exciting, more like.

He kissed me again. "Try me."

"I'll ask you that question again after I've told you a little story about my grandmother," I said.

"Baby, there's nothing you or anybody can tell me that'll make a damn bit of difference to the way I feel about you."

And somewhere in heaven, Grandma Parks smiled with satisfaction.

EPILOGUE

Mimi

"Say Mama."

"Dada."

I forced a smile. "This is really important to me, Junior. Come on, say, Ma...ma."

"Da...da," he chirped, and had the gall to grin toothlessly at me.

"Right. That's very good. Mommy is really proud of you. Now it's time to say, Mama. Come on, be a good boy and say Ma."

"Da."

"Junior, say Ma."

"Da."

"Say Mama for god's sake."

"Dada."

I took a deep breath. There must be another way. I walked over to the freezer and took out ice cream. I put it into a bowl and brought it back.

"Mmmm…ice cream. Say Mama."

He flung his hands around excitedly and stared at the ice cream.

I scraped a little into the spoon. "Now say Mama and I'll give you this ice cream."

I heard a sound and turned. Max was standing there with his eyebrows raised.

"Are you bribing our son so he will say your name first."

"No," I denied awkwardly.

"I just heard you."

I shrugged. "I was offering him ice cream."

"In exchange for him saying your name. That's called cheating, Mrs. Black."

"No, it's not. It's called being inventive."

I put the bowl of ice cream down and Junior suddenly screamed, "Mama."

For a second both of us froze then I clapped my hands with joy and danced around happily. "Did you hear that? Did you hear he called my name?" I came to a stop in front of Max and put my hand out. "I win. You lose. He said my name first. Cough up the five hundred dollars, buster."

He crossed his arms over his broad chest and stared at me. Oh my, my husband has a very, very nice chest.

"What?"

"Whose name did he say first?"

He stared at him incredulously. Surely, he wasn't going to pretend Junior said his name. "Mine. You heard it yourself. He said Mama."

"I forgot to mention that I stood outside the door for a few minutes before I actually decided to come in."

I took a step back. "Oh."

He shook his head in wonder. "I can't believe how competitive you are. You were going to let me believe that he said your name first, weren't you?"

"I would have eventually told you," I muttered.

"Really? When?"

"I don't know. At his graduation or something."

"Come here."

I walked up to him and he put his arms around me.

"Are you mad with me?" I asked.

"Nope."

I chewed my lower lip. "Why not?"

"Because you are the most delicious thing I ever laid eyes on. And there is nothing more entertaining than watching you blatantly lie and cheat just to win a bet."

I grinned. "That's not what you said about the first bet we took."

"When you poisoned me, you mean."

"It was not poison. It was just a laxative. Everybody needs to clean their system out now and again."

"Actually, it was a love potion," he said and kissed me. My husband knows how to kiss. He makes the rest of the world fall away.

THE END